"Do you ever think of our baby?"

"Addie."

"Do you, Skip?"

He looked away, sighed, turned back. "I'm so glad you asked. *So glad.* There's something I need to tell you." He lifted his eyes and a chill skimmed her spine.

"Do you know something? Do you know where she is? Is she all right?"

"Addie... Oh, God, how to say this... Addie, she's here in—"

"Here?" She tore her hand away, grabbed his arm. "What do you mean *here?* Where?" Her fingers clutched his T-shirt. *"Who—?"*

"It's Becky, Addie."

"No, I mean *our* baby. The one I...we..."

His eyes didn't waver. Those honey-gold eyes she had loved when she was fifteen, sixteen, seventeen.

Until he'd deserted her.

Dear Reader,

Two summers ago, I traveled to Bowen Island for a weekend writing retreat. A twenty-minute ferry ride from the mainland, the island harbors a small village with eclectic shops, restaurants and bed-and-breakfasts, while its rural interior hosts small farms of livestock, fruits and vegetables. In contrast, million-dollar homes dot the western shores. But what struck me most was the serenity the island offered.

And so an idea evolved about a fictitious island, which became my new miniseries HOME TO FIREWOOD ISLAND, in which three sisters—Addie, Lee and Kat— make peace with their pasts by finding happiness on their little island home.

Their Secret Child is Addie's story, and first in the series. I hope you enjoy her journey as she reunites with her high school sweetheart.

Mary

PS—For upcoming details about Lee's story, next in the series, check my Web site at www.maryjforbes.com.

THEIR
SECRET CHILD

MARY J. FORBES

Silhouette®

SPECIAL EDITION®

Published by Silhouette Books

America's Publisher of Contemporary Romance

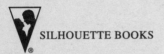

SILHOUETTE BOOKS

ISBN-13: 978-0-373-24902-2
ISBN-10:   0-373-24902-0

THEIR SECRET CHILD

Books by Mary J. Forbes

Silhouette Special Edition

A Forever Family #1625
A Father, Again #1661
Everything She's Ever Wanted #1702
Twice Her Husband #1755
The Man from Montana #1800
His Brother's Gift #1840
Red Wolf's Return #1858
*First-Time Valentine #1881
†Their Secret Child #1902

*The Wilder Family
†Home to Firewood Island

MARY J. FORBES

grew up on a prairie ranch where the skies were broad and blue, the hay fragrant, and the winters cold and snowy. Today, she lives with her family in the Pacific Northwest where she teaches school, writes her stories, nurtures her garden, and walks or jogs in any weather.

For R, V, K & J—
Love you all!

Chapter One

Today she would see him again—the first time in thirteen years.

Thirteen years. And she'd counted every one.

Not because of him. Never because of Skip Dalton.

If she'd thought of him at all in that span of time, it was because someone mentioned his name in passing or because Dempsey Malloy had loved to watch football.

But she was no longer married to Dempsey and football hadn't crossed her TV screen in over a year.

Truth be known, little crossed her TV screen these days. Any leisure time she had, she utilized by sewing, baking or caring for her bees—when she wasn't teaching or tutoring. And then there was her mother, who'd decided last spring to cut back her hours at the hair salon, which meant this summer Charmaine called her every "free" day and asked, "Whatcha doing?"

No, the thirteen years Addie had counted had been for another reason—a logical decision her father termed it.

Logical.

Forget emotion. Forget tears. Forget the hole in her soul that some nights threatened to kill her.

Decisions didn't cater to the weak-minded. Decisions meant logic—and Addie Malloy *lived* logic.

For a fleeting moment, her work-scarred fingers trembled at her left earlobe and she nearly dropped the tiny golden sunflower dangling on its fine chain.

God, why had she listened to her parents all those years ago?

Because you were a coward, Addie. Just as you are now, shaking in your boots, knowing you'll see him *again. Shaking like a little scaredy-cat.*

Clamping her bottom lip, she pushed the earring post firmly into place and uttered a sigh of relief when it was done. Should she add a bit of mascara to her stubby lashes? Her sisters, Lee and Kat, always demanded she should wear makeup, that mascara would augment her eyes, make them fab-u-lous.

But this wasn't a date and she wasn't going for Skip Dalton.

Stepping back from the bathroom mirror, she checked her face, her strong tanned arms, the yellow sundress that was a hand-me-down from Kat. It would have to do. *She* would have to do. Money wasn't a commodity on the island, especially Firewood Island with its two thousand souls, the majority of whose heritage heralded from the hippie sixties.

And as keeper of 480,000 bees she fit right in with the island's agriculturalists and minifarms, or "hobby farms" as some had the audacity to call them. Maintaining and nurturing twelve hives year-round wasn't a hobby. It was damned hard work.

She pulled her unruly hair—dirty blond hair, she'd always thought—into a thick knot on her head, shoved in four long pins to hold the mass in place and ignored the flyaway strands creeping free around her face. Not her best attribute, her hair. No, *that* would be her mouth. Her downfall at sixteen—and again at twenty-two.

Closer to the mirror, she scrutinized the absence of lines, creases or thinning. Thank God. Thirty-one and holding. Her lips remained full and feminine and youthful and…a little wanton. Maybe even sexy if she applied a trace of pink. She would not let *him* think she'd been kitchen-bound these past years with a passel of kids clamoring around her ankles.

Her heart lurched. *You don't need a houseful, Addie. Michaela embodies every one of your dreams.*

Still, she couldn't stop the ache that stabbed her chest. Thirteen years of memories bleeding out of a black mist like a herd of fire-snorting dragons. God, why today of all days?

She knew why—Skip Dalton.

Forget him! You did it before, you can do it now.

Right. That's why her heart hammered and a flush spread up her neck. *Don't be an idiot. He won't recognize you, anyway.*

Holding tight to that notion, she shut off the bathroom light and stepped into the hallway.

In her daughter's bedroom, seven-year-old Michaela sat on the floor, changing the apparel of three of her ten Barbies.

Her little sneakers were on the wrong feet again, and her left sock was missing. Addie noted the clothes Michaela had pulled on: a yellow T-shirt that was inside out and pink shorts. These days, neon pink and sunshine-yellow were prize contenders in her tiny fashion world. And she'd attempted to snap four pink barrettes at precarious angles into her dark ringlets.

Addie forced herself to remain calm, not to rush in, crush her baby to her heart, drink in her child's scent. "Ready to see Gram, honeykins?"

"'Kay." Scooping the dolls into her arms, her daughter scrambled to her feet and caught Addie's hand.

"You'll have tons of fun making cookies with Gram." Gently, she swung their hands. "Better than what Mommy's having at the high school and that boring party."

"Yeah."

She wished her little girl would talk more. The school psychologist was trying, but it would take months of patience and a variety of strategies, Addie knew, before her baby would come out of the funk she'd fallen into with Dempsey's departure fourteen months ago.

Outside on the wooden stoop shaded by three western hemlocks towering over her turn-of-the-century carriage-style house she hesitated a moment and looked down her long lane and across the road. A big new house stood almost completed and barely visible amidst the lush growth of red cedars, ash, Douglas fir and Garry oaks. Painted white with green trim and shutters, the building jutted up two stories, showcasing a turret at one end and a massive stone fireplace at the other. An expansive wraparound porch enclosed the entire structure like a small moat.

Observing the construction for the past two months, Addie had heard rumors in the village of Burnt Bend about the owner. Some rich guy, they said, looking for a summer place.

If he was rich, why hadn't he built on the water where he could moor his yacht? Why here, on a piece of property dense with woods and creeks, and down a rural road out in the middle of nowhere?

Well, it wasn't her affair. She didn't care who lived in the house, as long as they minded their own business and the quiet returned. She was tired of the hammering and sawing, the constant buzz of power tools, the coming and going of trucks. She wanted the peace of the woods again, the song of birds waking her at dawn, the deer visiting her backyard.

With a sigh, she looked down at her daughter. "Go on, honey, get in the truck while Mommy locks the door." On the faint, early August breeze, Addie heard Charmaine's cynicism: *No one locks doors around here. Why do you?*

"Because, Mom," she whispered, watching Michaela climb into the Dodge Dakota, "I don't trust Dempsey." Though she'd never tell Charmaine Wilson that. Her mother favored Addie's ex-husband, thought he should have time to sort things out in his head, to "find himself." Which was what he'd told Addie the day he walked out of their lives. According to Charmaine, Dempsey was just a "mixed-up kid."

Interesting turn of phrase for a man of forty-two. But not surprising, coming from a mother who had told Addie thirteen years ago to "grow up" when she'd found herself pregnant in high school.

With the divorce from Dempsey finalized last January, Addie had moved to her dad's "homestead" house—three miles from Burnt Bend—and installed new locks. She had no intention of letting her globe-trotting ex back in her life or her house.

Today, however, she wanted to install a dead bolt. On her heart.

She would need it when she watched Harry McLane transfer his three-decades-old title as coach of the high school football team to Skip Dalton, his former student.

And her first love.

Skip Dalton. Back to stay. Back where she'd no doubt run in to him at the post office, the coffee shop, his mother's grocery store. Skip Dalton, hero on the mainland, and now on Firewood Island. *Again.*

She couldn't win no matter how hard she tried.

The school gym and the grounds out the side doors were crowded with students, current and past.

People had come from places as far away as San Francisco and Cheyenne to honor the coach for whom they had cheered and/or run yards, caught field passes and scored touchdowns on the Fire High football field. Thirty years of history had happened between those posts and on those bleachers. Skip should know. From the field, he had waved and grinned at the girls sitting in those bleachers.

And that, unfortunately, had been the start of *his* history.

He stood beside Coach at the door, greeting folks he hadn't

spoken to in thirteen years. People he'd last seen as kids, and who now had kids of their own. Some former schoolmates had gained weight. One guy was bald, while three were salt-and-pepper gray.

But the girls, the *women*—he had to blink a couple times to recognize even the smallest familiarity. Not until they'd said their names had he remembered. *Ah, yes,* Alicia Wells and…was that Francie—aka Fancy Torres? And Elise Haply and…

He regretted not recognizing the women the way he did the men. 'Course, he'd played ball with twenty-five of the guys during his high school years, shared locker jokes, showers, training techniques, victories and losses but, hell, he'd dated damn near as many girls back then.

Admittedly, at one time or other, he'd likely dated every woman standing around today chatting, laughing and sipping punch. Many—when their eyes collided with his—gave him cool, distant looks. No, they hadn't forgotten his cocky attitude as quarterback of Fire High.

Today, they likely detected the *I don't remember you* in his eyes when he looked their way or was introduced to them. That had to hurt, to know they'd been about as important to him as the socks on his feet.

Not something he was proud of. *Hell.* If history could be re-written, he'd erase his entire senior year and begin again.

To right the wrongs he'd done to *her.*

For that chance, he'd give up his nine years of pro ball.

But the past was gone and all he had at the moment was what he could do for his old high school. Give something back the way he hadn't been able to for Addie.

"Skip, you remember Cheryl Mosley?" Beside him, Coach McLane touched the elbow of a tall brunette. "She married Keith Bartley. Remember Keith, our water boy? Cheryl's head of our science department and will be splitting eleventh-grade chem with you."

Skip nodded to the woman. Fortunately, he'd completed his

science degree before going pro. While football had been his love, he'd known it could die in a second on the field. And it had two years ago with a damaged left shoulder from a downward drive by a linebacker of the opposing team. So here he stood, suit and tie intact, counting his lucky stars in more ways than one to be taking over Coach McLane's chemistry classes and the football team.

Smiling, he shook the woman's hand. Cheryl. Yeah, he remembered her. She'd led the cheerleaders in chants and dance steps at every game in his days on the Fire High team.

He had dated her for five months. The longest relationship he'd had on the island. Before he met Addie Wilson.

Addie, whom he had yet to see.

She's not coming, a taunting little voice whispered in his ear. *Why should she? You dumped her. Left her high and dry. No, make that big and alone.*

"I look forward to working with you, Skip," Cheryl's voice hauled him back into the celebration. "We'll have to get together before school starts for some planning. Now that Coach is leaving," she said with a sad smile, before turning her gaze back to Skip, "we'll need to make some changes in the science department."

He had no idea what changes she meant, but she stated it with such chilly professionalism, that all he could do was nod a second time. "Sure, anytime. I won't be in the phone book yet, but Coach'll have my number."

Moving away, she issued an indifferent, "Great. Meantime, welcome aboard."

"Thanks."

When she'd gone, another took her place and so it went— staff, former students, parents of attending students, kids already on the football team. One after the other, they patted Coach on the back, wiped tears over the old man's retirement…and greeted Skip with lukewarm enthusiasm. The adage that women have long memories pricked like a thorn.

He had no illusion to the length of Addie Wilson's memory.

An hour later, the stream entering the gym thinned as the chairs filled and it was time for the presentations and announcements. Principal Jeff Holby introduced Skip as a member of the school staff before Coach McLane slung an arm around his shoulder and took the mike.

"I'm thrilled," the retiring teacher said, "to be passing the torch onto such a fine young man as Skip Dalton. He grew up on Firewood Island, attended its schools and went out into the world to make a name for our little spot on the map." Grinning at Skip, he continued, "As a quarterback in the NFL, no less. Doggone it, but that makes me mighty proud."

A few whistles shrilled, with a spattering of applause. More for Coach's delight, Skip knew, than for *his* meritorious career.

"After thirty years," Coach went on, "I can't think of one person more suitable to take over for me." Stepping back, he held out the keys to the locker rooms and coaching office. "Skip, these are yours now. Make the team yours. Make the wins yours. We're behind you every yard and run of the way."

This time the crowd's applause rang to the rafters. The words *Coach McLane* were chanted throughout the room for almost five minutes, before they shifted slowly to *Coach Dalton*.

And that's when he saw Addie.

She stood at the back of the gym, on the periphery of a group that had come in late. She wasn't clapping and chanting, but instead she leaned against the wall with her arms crossed, a purse slung over a shoulder…and watched him. He couldn't help grin. The din ebbed into the distance, and it was all he could do not to jump off the stage and stride across the room.

He wanted to see her up close. He wanted to touch her hand, her soft tawny hair and look into those summer blue eyes. Say her name…

And what…? Beg forgiveness? Tell her what you've done, why you're here, what you hope to achieve?

Concerning her, what *did* he hope to gain?

The question had burned Skip's brain since he'd made the decision ten months ago to relocate back to his hometown. At the time, he hadn't consciously thought about the answer. Hearing of Coach McLane's retirement, he had called the school, talked to Coach, then Principal Holby and later, the school board. Each had jumped at the chance of having him procure the position of Fire High's senior coach, and before he gave it an ounce of thought, he'd signed a five-year contract.

For his daughter, first and foremost.

His gaze slipped to where twelve-year-old Becky sat in the front row, blue eyes sparkling as she offered a thumbs-up. His chest hurt with a love he couldn't fathom. God, every time he looked at the girl, he couldn't believe his luck in finding her—and getting her back.

The only regret Skip had was for the loss of previous years. But this was now and, dammit, the girl deserved a kind and loving home, a great school and community, but most of all, a family to whom she could attach a sense of belonging.

In Skip's mind that was achievable on Firewood Island with Addie.

Though he'd have to tread with care there.

Oh, yeah. From what he'd heard through the gossip mill in the two days he'd been back, she was a woman of independent means. And a loner.

Looking at her across the gym, he could imagine that stubborn tilt to her chin. The one that said, *I'm here for Coach, not you.*

Finally the applause died. Skip said a few words of gratitude and appreciation, then the ceremonies were over. Time to work the crowd, chat up his goals for the upcoming year and hope to introduce his daughter around.

And meet Addie. Before all else, introduce Becky to Addie.

His daughter waited at the bottom of the stage steps. "You were great up there, Dad. They're gonna love you as coach."

Her confidence bowled him over, never mind how easily "*Dad*" slipped into her sentences. When he explained his relationship to her ten months ago, Becky—desperate for family—had taken the news and change with a faith that had broken his heart. Skip hoped that same faith would withstand the test when he told Addie about her daughter.

He put a hand on his child's shoulder. "We'll see, honey. I didn't leave here on the best of terms, remember?" In small increments over the past months, he'd explained as much as he could about himself. But not about Addie. No, that part of his history he hadn't the guts to disclose. Yet.

"So you've said." Becky's smile was the moon. "But, hey, once you win a game, the town'll be so happy to have you."

Skip chuckled. "We can only hope. Want a hot dog?"

They headed for the side doors. Over Becky's dark head, Skip searched the room for Addie, for that pretty yellow dress, but she was nowhere to be seen. Had he imagined her in the rear crowd? Probably. She'd been on his mind for months.

Since he'd found Becky.

Admit it, Addie's been in your head since you left thirteen years ago.

For half his life, she had been in his nightmares, and his dreams. Well, it was time. Time to come full circle.

Determined, he touched his daughter's elbow. "Let's go scrounge up some food."

They walked into the island's sea-scented sunshine.

Sometimes, it amazed Addie that five people had once slept, ate, laughed, opened birthday and Christmas presents, fought over bathroom privileges and closets and clothes…and survived in the cramped six-room structure in which her mother still lived.

Pulling the truck into the dirt lane of her childhood home on the outskirts of town, she thought of her sisters Lee and Kat living elsewhere on the island. Of the three, Addie visited their mother almost daily; Lee was frequently off island in her plane and Kat was tied up with the Country Cabin, her bed-and-breakfast.

As to their fathers, well, they were another story.

Addie's died two years ago and Lee's had left when she was a child. And Kat's… No one knew who or where Kat's daddy was, or if he even lived.

Mom's closet secret. That's what Kat called Charmaine's unwillingness to reveal the past.

"What's the point? It's done and gone." Their mother's favorite battle cry whenever one of them pressed for the name.

Done and gone. *Well, Mom,* Addie thought, *here's a news flash. Sometimes done and gone comes back to bite you in the butt.*

Skip Dalton was a living example.

Standing at the back of the gym, seeing him for the first time in more than a decade, hearing that smooth, deep voice… God, she'd been a teenager again and he the school jock, the team quarterback, the college student come home for Christmas. The boy kissing her under the school bleachers, touching her in places no one had touched, taking her virginity in his pickup truck on the shore of the island's Silver Lake, and finally… making a baby with her. In this house, in her old bedroom, thirty feet from where she sat this minute in her aged truck.

Pushing off the memories, she opened the door and jumped down. Time to get her child and go home and let Skip Dalton go to whomever wanted him. Which likely would be half the women on the island.

Addie released a soft snort. He'd best take care because those women now had husbands.

And that stopped him before?

Climbing the steps to her mother's door, she shook her head. Not according to the sports commentators. Wasn't it four years ago that Skip dated a woman recently separated from her husband—not divorced, separated—and the man had come after him with a shotgun?

Yes, Addie remembered Dempsey talking about it while he watched a game, and laughing about Skip Dalton looking a "little green around the gills" when he was interviewed about the incident. Addie hadn't watched the interview; instead she'd walked into the kitchen to clean out the dishwasher. The last thing she needed was Skip Dalton's face filling the TV screen and Dempsey giggling over the whole tasteless affair.

So goes the life of the rich and fabulous, she thought, knocking on her mother's door.

A moment later, it opened. Charmaine stood on the threshold and Addie blinked back Skip Dalton's image.

"Hey, Mom." She stepped into the familiar entranceway with its cabbage-rose mat and wooden bar of coat hooks on the wall. The scent of chocolate-chip cookies permeated the air; grandma and granddaughter had been busy the past hour. "How's my baby?"

"Fine." Closing the door, Charmaine scrutinized Addie's face. "You look as if you've seen your father's ghost."

"I wish." She moved down the tiny hallway and into the living quarters where Michaela crawled under a blue blanket held in place by several books between the sofa and coffee table. Three Barbies and a Ken lay on the carpet near the "house" entrance. Addie tugged gently on her daughter's leg. "Hey, button. Ready for home?"

Michaela peeked from under the coverlet. "C-c-can I s-s-stay?" Brown eyes pleading, she crouched farther under the blanket tent. Addie understood. Her child had built the house and now wanted playtime.

Kneeling on the floor, she took her daughter's hands. "Speak slowly, honey."

"Can...I...stay?"

"Gram has some stuff to do this afternoon, Michaela." Addie wasn't sure of her mother's commitments, but *she* needed to feel the security of her own house. She needed to know that her world wasn't about to turn upside down now that Skip Dalton was back.

Michaela pouted. "But…I want…to…play."

"I know, button. Maybe we'll come back tomorrow, okay?" Addie held out a hand, signaling the matter was done.

The child gathered the dolls into her pink knapsack and climbed to her feet. "'B-bye, Gram."

Charmaine tucked a packet of cookies into her granddaughter's small hand. "These are for you, but Mom will give you permission when you can have one."

"'Kay."

She kissed Michaela's hair. "See you later, darlin'."

As Addie ushered her daughter out of the house, Charmaine whispered, "What happened at Harry's retirement party that's got you in a dither?"

"Nothing. The new coach was introduced and Harry got the token plaque and gold watch. End of story."

"Was Skip Dalton there?"

Addie turned to Charmaine as Michaela scrambled into the truck. "Don't act as if you didn't know, Mom. The paper carried the announcement twice."

Charmaine's eyes narrowed. "Did you talk to him?"

"No."

"But you saw him."

"I saw him."

Questions burned in Charmaine's eyes. *What did he look like? Is he still handsome? Were people impressed? Has he changed?* Ten thousand questions that meant nothing—and everything.

"I have to go." Addie moved down the steps.

"Addie… Your father didn't mean for you to be so hurt over…it."

It. A tiny word for the life-changing events that occurred the second Cyril Wilson began brainwashing his daughter to give up the man she loved, and then later to give up their baby.

She turned, faced her mother. "Do not go there, Mom. I know why Dad pushed so hard. He didn't want his precious daughter dragged into the trailer trash bin."

Charmaine's eyes widened, her mouth fell open. "Oh, Addie. That wasn't it at all. He wanted you to have a chance, he wanted—"

"Exactly. He wanted. Whatever he wanted he got."

Her mother came down the steps. "That's just not true."

"Isn't it?"

"Your father did what he thought was best—"

"For who? Me? You? Our family? Don't kid yourself. Dad was into saving face in this town. You know it, I know it. Lee and Kat know it. Everyone knows except you. When are you going to own up to that fact?"

"You're letting Skip get to you, Adelina, and he's not worth it."

Addie scoffed a laugh. "He must be worth something. At one time he was the best quarterback in the league."

Her mother cast a sideways glance. Guilt probably. Well, Addie no longer cared how Charmaine felt. Throughout the past decade she'd grown a prickly spine, one Dempsey had walked into a time or two.

"Were your sisters there?" her mother asked.

"I didn't see them. I left the second Coach got his gold watch."

Charmaine sighed.

"What? Did you expect me to hang around, bump into Skip and then throw out a welcome mat?" Her eyes narrowed. "God, Mother. You did." Addie opened the truck's door. She couldn't get away from this conversation fast enough.

"You'll be teaching at the same school," Charmaine pointed out.

"Which I do not look forward to."

"Why don't you try breaking the ice first? Maybe talking to him will help with the issues you've kept inside."

"*Issues?* When Dad pushed me to sign those papers, I wanted to die. *Die,* do you understand?" Issues, indeed.

"M-M-Mommy," Michaela called anxiously from inside the truck.

"Look, I'll see you later."

Charmaine hurried forward. "What're you going to do about—"

"Absolutely nothing. The man means zilch to me." She got in, turned the ignition—and left her mother in the driveway.

Nothing, zilch, nada. Remember that, Addie.

Skip Dalton was a pebble in the road of her life. Easily kicked aside. *Then why are you so annoyed?* And worried.

Chapter Two

The following Monday, Skip drove his Toyota pickup down the wooded driveway leading to his new home and parked beside his Prius. Yesterday, the movers had brought all the furniture; today he and Becky would arrange and unpack the boxes.

Standing in the morning sunshine, he grinned across the truck's hood. "Well, Bean. This is it. This is home now." Skip hoped the girl would like the house, the island, the school she'd be attending after the Labor Day weekend in a few weeks. He watched her gaze at the structure gleaming in the morning light, her mouth slightly open, eyes as round as pizzas.

"It's amazing. I've never been in a house this big. Is it just for us?"

"Just us." For now. He couldn't predict the future, but he hoped he and the lady across the road could eventually become friends for Becky's sake. After that…who knew?

"Look," he said, embarrassed suddenly by her awe. It *was,* after all, just a house. One of three he owned, and not the biggest. "If you want to scout around, I'll start inside. Come in when you're ready."

Her expression was grateful. "I'd like that. It's so quiet here. I never realized it, but I like the sound of…"

"Nature?"

"Yeah." The word blew out on a little huff as she observed an American goldfinch pick at the bark of an old Garry oak in the front yard.

Skip smiled. "The island may be small, honey, and a good portion may have burned to ashes in 1892, but it's all grown back, including the wildlife, so enjoy it." Happy to let her explore the premises, he walked up the porch steps to open the front door.

For the first time in over a decade he had come home.

Becky wandered around the property. The air was so fresh and clean and the trees were incredibly green and grand and gorgeous. As if she stood in Narnia during summertime.

She wanted to pinch herself to make sure she wasn't dreaming. Was it only ten months ago that her dad found her?

It seemed like yesterday. And forever.

Man, her *real* dad…

He was so cool. Kind and patient and just plain *nice*. And he occasionally called her Bean 'cause she was growing like a bean sprout, he said. When she thought of her other dad… Skip was so different than…*him*.

She was glad Jesse, as she'd begun to think of him, was in the Walla Walla prison. She swallowed back the ache in her throat at the thought of her mom. Becky couldn't believe she'd been gone almost four years. She tried to picture the woman she'd loved so much.

Mom, with her soft blond hair and sweet smile.

Mom, reading to her just before bedtime.

Mom, helping with her homework.

The images swam across Becky's mind… Except her mom

seemed hazy, the way a person looked standing in a really thick fog. And when she tried to remember her mother's voice, there was nothing, not a single word.

Maybe it was best this way. Maybe forgetting her mom's face would help her forget the horror of *that day*.

She swung around and realized she'd almost walked into the forest. *Jeez, Becks. Focus on this life. Your new life. Don't think of then.*

Hurrying to the front yard, Becky saw the road they'd traveled coming from the village. Across it, up a long dirt trail was a green cottage, and on its stoop sat a child.

They had to be the neighbors. Maybe the family had kids her age. Like one of the girls she'd met last week at the retirement ceremony.

Eager to begin new friendships, Becky walked down her dad's driveway and across the road.

"Hi," she called as she went up their lane.

The kid wore a pink top and shorts. Above each ear was a dark pigtail that hung down her skinny arms. She looked about six or seven. And a little scared. As she got closer, Becky said, "I'm Becky, your new neighbor."

The girl had big brown eyes. Her mouth worked, but nothing came out. Becky plopped on the stoop next to a row of Barbie dolls.

"Hey." She picked up a queenlike version. "I had a Princess Barbie a long time ago. But then my mom died and I had to move and I lost Princess." Becky rocked the doll, humming a little tune. The child gave her the sweetest smile she'd ever seen. "What's your name?" she asked.

"M-M-Michaela."

Becky acted as if she heard stuttering all the time. "Pretty name."

The kid's smile showed two missing front teeth. "M-M-Mommy n' me are g-g-gonna check the b-b-bees. Wanna c-c-come?"

Bees? Becky looked around. "There's a hive somewhere?"

"Uh-huh. Mom s-s-sells the honey."

"*Ohhh.* You mean, she has those white bee boxes?"

Sunshine dipped into the girl's eyes, making them as gold as honey. "I can…ask…Mom…if you…can…come see them."

"Hey, that'd be cool."

The door behind them opened. "Michaela?" A skinny woman in jeans and blue t-shirt looked down at them.

The child scrambled up to grab the woman's hand. "Mom, this is B-B-Becky. She's our n-n-neighbor." She pointed. "Over there."

Becky got to her feet. "I didn't mean to trespass, ma'am."

"You didn't." The woman had a soft voice. Her hand stroked her daughter's curly pigtails and for a second Becky remembered her own mother's fingers sifting through her hair in the same way.

"B-B-Becky likes Princess best, j-j-just l-l-like me."

"Slow down, button."

Becky smiled. "I get nervous meeting new people, too."

The alertness in the woman's face eased. "I'm Addie Malloy."

"I'm Becky Dalton."

Ms. Malloy's eyebrows crashed. "You're Skip Dalton's *daughter?*"

"Yes." Was that bad? "Do you know him?"

The woman stared at her for so long Becky shuffled her feet. Then Ms. Malloy looked toward their house and her eyes got really cold. "Yeah," she said. "I know Mr. Dalton."

Oh, man. Their neighbor didn't like her dad. Why? She started to back away. Had she heard about her past? Becky wondered. No, her dad would never tell. "I should go. My dad's probably wondering where I am. It was really nice meeting you. 'Bye, Mick."

"It's Michaela." Frost hung in the woman's voice. "She doesn't like Mick."

"Oops." Becky couldn't stop a nervous giggle. "Sorry." Leaving the pair standing on the sunny stoop, she hurried down the path among the trees.

Sheesh. Wasn't that always the way? A cute kid with a mean mother... Poor girl. Becky knew what it was like to live with a parent who wasn't kind or friendly. Yet, Ms. Malloy had *seemed* kind, patting the girl's hair. But maybe that was for show. Maybe she was why Michaela stuttered. Maybe the girl was dying for friends, but Ms. Malloy didn't want people hanging around. Becky peeked over her shoulder.

The steps were empty.

She broke into a run.

Skip put his shoulder into the shove that slid his sleigh bed into place. He wanted the bed facing the windows across the hardwood. That way, first thing every morning he'd look straight into the stand of evergreens circling his property. Almost done with arranging the bedroom furniture, he heard the front door open.

"Dad?"

Dad. A shiver darted through Skip. He still had a hard time accepting how easily his daughter had taken to him. Twelve years she'd been under someone else's care. His own flesh and blood. What an idiot he'd been to allow such a precious commodity to be handed over to strangers. What had he been thinking to listen to his father's rants about one-in-a-million chances and how Skip needed to stop feeling sorry for something that wasn't his fault?

Except it had been his fault. He'd been nineteen, Addie only seventeen when he'd gotten her pregnant that Christmas. Much as he hated the truth, he had forfeited his child for a mere *chance.* He could push the blame onto his father until the cows came home, but the fact was, at the end of the day, *he'd* made the choice.

If he could erase the past, if he could just begin again, give Becky a new childhood, one with him and possibly Addie...

All the ifs in the world won't change a damn thing, Skip.

"Dad?" She thundered up the stairs.

"In here, Bean," he called. He started the nickname within days of seeing her for the first time, a tall, gangly girl with his dark hair and long, narrow feet.

She flung around the doorjamb, her cheeks flushed. "I met the neighbors across the road. Ms. Malloy and her girl, Michaela."

Ah, hell. Skip crossed the room. "Becky, next time let me know before you leave the property, okay?"

"Why? Is there something wrong with them?" She cut a glance toward the window.

"No." Only thirteen years of abandonment by him. "We live in the country and I'd rather you didn't go somewhere without telling me." He tried to soften his anxiety with a smile. "It'll keep me from worrying."

"Jesse never cared where I went."

Jesse Farmer, her adopted dad. "I'm not Jesse, honey." He brushed the too-long bangs from her eyes. "Look, I'm still learning the family thing, so bear with me, okay? If I'm a little paranoid it just means I need to know you're okay." *That no one is hurting you anymore.*

With a shrug she wandered to his clothing boxes stacked near the closet's open door. Peering inside, she said, "I don't think we'll be friends with them anyway."

"No?"

"Ms. Malloy isn't…very friendly."

"In what way?" Had Addie slammed the door in Becky's face?

Another shrug. "She seems…uptight. Maybe it's because her daughter stutters and stuff."

He'd heard about Addie having another child, one from the man she divorced seven months ago.

"How do you know she stutters?"

"She was sitting on their front step when I went over, and we were chatting about her dolls when the mom came outside."

"Oh."

Becky looked over her shoulder. "The little girl's really cute—and shy. And she has these big brown eyes. I think her mom is overprotective because of the way she talks." Suddenly, her face brightened. "Hey, maybe we can ask them over for dinner in a couple days and—"

"Whoa, whoa." Skip brought up his hands. "Let's take it one day at a time, Bean. We've got a lot to do around here first." Primarily, he needed to get reacquainted with the lady in question. "How about we wait a few days, see where we're at with the unpacking." He inclined his head toward the door. "You haven't even checked out your room yet."

Which told him how much neighbors and friends meant to his daughter. The "friends" she'd had in the trailer park in Lynnwood—where her family had lived—Skip wished she'd never met.

Becky rushed into the hallway, bent on her assignment. "Which room is mine?"

He leaned in the doorway. "There are four, so take your pick."

"I can? No way!"

He watched her dash into each, listened to her "oohs" and "aahs" as she toured their confines, until in the last and farthest from his room, he heard, "This one! I'm picking this one."

He was grinning when she poked her head from the doorway. "Is that okay?"

"Yup, it's yours. And so are these boxes." He walked to five piled in the corridor, hoisted two into his arms. When they had carried them in, he said, "Have at it, honey. Decorate it any way you want."

She flung her arms around him in a quick, rare hug. "Thanks, Dad."

"My pleasure." He walked to the doorway. "You going to be

okay for a bit? I'd like to wander over and introduce myself to Ms. Malloy and her daughter. Might as well find out now if I'll need to plant a twenty-foot wall in front of my house."

Her eyes were apprehensive. "Really?"

Skip laughed. "Just kidding, Bean."

"Oh. Want me to come?" She looked longingly around her room.

"No. You have fun. I'll be back in two shakes." He started down the hallway.

"Dad?" She peered around the doorjamb.

"Yeah."

"Don't let Ms. Malloy scare you."

"Why? Is she ugly?" From what he'd seen across the school gym last week, she looked as he remembered. Petite and pretty.

Becky shook her head. "Her eyes are mean."

He couldn't imagine it. Addie had the prettiest, bluest eyes he'd ever seen. And they gazed at him every day from Becky's dear face.

All through lunch, the memory of Skip's daughter smiling at Michaela dug like a sliver into Addie's thoughts. He had a *daughter* who looked like him. Who was almost the age *their* child would have been. Wasting time had obviously not been a priority in Skip Dalton's life. How incredibly dumb she'd been to presume he had mourned the loss of their child. Instead, he immediately found someone else and— She slammed the last rinsed lunch plate onto the drying rack and bit her tongue to keep from screaming.

Some rich guy looking for a summer place. Too late she associated the chitchat in Burnt Bend regarding the house in the trees across Clover Road....

He had been that guy.

Such a fool she was, keeping her head in the sand, shunning gossip. She hated it at seventeen when she found herself pregnant, and she hated it today, but sometimes, dammit, she should listen. On rare occasions that grapevine fed vital information.

A laugh welled in her throat—before anger, dislike and hurt surged forth. *Damn him.*

He would have known she lived within shouting distance. He would have investigated his neighbors, the area surrounding his land. A successful and affluent man like Skip Dalton would have taken precautionary steps before moving into a community, especially a rural community where trees and three-hundred-yard driveways concealed houses from view. He was money now. Barrels of money.

"Mommy?" Michaela spoke at her side.

Cool head, Addie. Your *daughter is all that matters.* "What, angel?"

"Can I lick s-s-some honey off a s-s-spoon after we check the b-b-bees?"

"Oh, button." Addie cupped her child's face, kissed her silky hair. "You bet." And just like that the hurt in her heart eased. "Go to the washroom, then we'll head out."

"Yay!"

Smiling, she watched the child run from the kitchen. Michaela loved honey—such a natural source of nourishment—and, amazingly, was not afraid of the hives.

Michaela, she thought. Her baby, her reason for living.

Two minutes later, she led the way down the path to the wooden honey shed where she kept their "spacemen" suits, as Michaela called the white coveralls they wore to attend the hives, and where, in an hour, she would be melting the wax off the honeycombs with a hot knife before running the honey.

For years, Addie's father operated eighty hives, but Addie's main responsibility was Michaela. Added to that was the high school where she'd begun teaching again after her divorce. So last winter, she had reduced the apiary to twelve hives. Eight on a red clover field three miles down the road, and four on a neighboring cucumber-squash patch. Although she harvested the bulk of the honey the first week of August, the clover bees would continue to produce until Labor Day.

She was stacking the fresh frames—combs in which bees produced harvestable honey—when Michaela darted for the shed door. "Mom! I f-f-forgot F-F-Felicity."

Chuckling, Addie handed her daughter the house key. "Can't have that, button. Don't forget to lock up when you come out."

From the time Michaela was old enough to come along, Addie had set the rule that only one doll came for the trip when they went to see the bees, and that doll remained secured in the truck's cab away from the insects.

As Michaela rushed down the path toward the back door, Addie headed for the pickup with their coveralls and gear: hive tool, smoker and the last stack of fresh frames.

That'd be so cool, Becky Dalton had told Michaela when she asked if the girl wanted to see the hives thirty minutes ago.

How old was she? Eleven, twelve? What did it matter?

A lot, dammit!

He'd moved on without a second's thought after telling Addie how much he loved her, and that nothing short of death would keep them apart. *Lying rat.* God, how could she have been so stupid?

"Arrgh!"

Rehashing the memories, she wanted to scream and stamp her feet.

A thought had her stumbling. What if he'd gotten a college girl pregnant around the same time he and Addie—

Oh, God. Her heart hurt. How often had she stood at the edge of that game field over the years and looked up at the bleachers? And remembered.

Remembered sitting among the hundreds of cheering students, watching the boy in the black-and-gold Fire High uniform take charge of his team.

How many times had she wondered if their baby had his eyes or mouth or those crazy elongated lashes? Whether she was tall or short, dark or blond? If she had his runners' legs?

Most of all, she wondered if the child knew how badly Addie had wanted her. And failed her.

She threw the gear into the bed of the truck harder than necessary, then reached down to the stack of frames on the ground. *Forgive me, little one.*

A shadow fell across her face. From the corner of her eye she caught sight of a pair of ratty men's sneakers.

"Hello, Addie."

Her heart slammed her ribs. His voice. So familiar and at one time so beloved. She couldn't move, couldn't move an inch. *He's here* was her only thought. *Right here.*

Slowly she rose; turned.

He stood two strides away, hands shoved into the pockets of a pair of tan cargo shorts. He'd always been tall, but today, this moment, *thirteen years after,* he loomed over her five-foot-four stature.

On occasion she had glimpsed his face on TV, noted the transformation of boy to man. Where once he held girls in thrall, today he undoubtedly did the same to women. Not because he was handsome, but because he exuded an elemental roughness manifested by those hewed cheeks and jaw, those dark brows, that hawkish nose.

A breeze riffled the flip of brown hair on his wide forehead and a memory speared up. There was a time she had trailed her fingers through that lock. A time she'd loved its texture.

"It's been a long while," he said when she continued to stare.

She gathered her scrambled thoughts. "What do you want, Skip?"

Imperceptibly, his shoulder lifted. "Just to say hi."

"And now you have."

"I'm...um..." He looked around her front yard. His eyes

were still that rich honey color, she noticed. Full of deep, dark mystery.

On a gesture to the big house she watched rise from the earth over the past three months, he said, "My daughter and I moved in across the road today."

Disregarding her pattering heart, she picked up two supers—square boxes housing the honeycomb frames—and carefully set them inside the truck.

"Yes," she said. "I noticed the moving trucks earlier, and... Becky met my daughter." She couldn't help emphasizing *my*. His daughter looked like him, the way Michaela looked like Dempsey. But, dammit, no matter how the cards fell, Michaela was *her* daughter.

My daughter. Mine.

Leaning down, he grabbed the second stack of honey frames. "I know. That's why I came over. I wanted to make sure she didn't cause trouble."

So. This visit wasn't to reacquaint them or introduce his family to hers. He was here to make sure he wouldn't be considered a lousy parent for having an intrusive daughter.

How like Skip. His name suited him after all. Skipping town thirteen years ago and now skipping back without a qualm, without a single concern that he'd nearly killed her with his brush-off.

Did he even care that she'd suffered twenty-three hours of labor, that she'd died a million deaths when they whisked her baby away in the time it took her to inhale a single breath?

Do you know I still wonder where she is?

"I have work to do," she said, seizing the frames from his hands. "And you have your family to go back to."

His wife, no doubt, would be wondering what he was doing across the road at the neighbor's house. The neighbor dressed in thready jeans, a long-sleeved T-shirt and old leather boots. On a blistering hot day.

"It's just Becky and me," he said. "And she's fixing her room.

You know how girls are. They… They fuss over…" He stepped back when he saw her eyes narrow. "Stuff." His hands found his hip pockets. "Addie, I…"

She shook her head. "No. This is not old home week. I do not want you coming around here, Skip." *Telling me about your child, your life.* His mouth opened and she held up a hand. "It's not up for discussion. You made your choice long ago. Let's leave it at that."

"I'm sorry."

She released a sharp laugh. "For what? For coming back to the island? For walking up my drive? For your daughter showing up on my doorstep?"

He blinked. "For everything." His throat worked a swallow. "From the beginning."

If he didn't leave soon, she'd throw a loaded box of honey frames at his head. "Please, go home. Go back to your… mansion, to your…whatever it is you do." On a mission, she marched to the honey shed for another load before she realized she'd finished and had locked the door.

Never mind, she'd find something else inside.

Shortening his stride, he kept an easy pace beside her. She had read about his shattered shoulder, the one ending his star-hung career despite five operations.

She damn well wouldn't feel sorry for him.

"Addie, we're going to be neighbors. For a long time. I'm not moving. Can't we put the past behind us?"

Whirling around, she looked up into those mellow eyes with their silly stretchy lashes. "Now, there's an idea. Can you tell me how it's done? How do you forget the past, Skip? You're a whiz at it, aren't you? Is it one of those twelve baby-step procedures?" She hated being catty, but the last thing on her radar was this man's feelings.

Again, the long-lashed blink. "You've changed."

"Damn right I have. It's called growing up." She rammed

the key into the shed's lock, flung open the door. "You should try it."

"You think my life's been a barrel of laughs?"

She heard the pinch of anger. "I don't give a flying rat's rump about your life. As long as it doesn't interfere with mine, we're good to go."

He stopped in the doorway, succinctly blocking a portion of natural light. Reluctantly, she noticed his nut-brown hair needed a good trimming.

He said, "I understand you teach at Fire High." The anger was gone, replaced with a softness she did not want to examine.

From a shelf, Addie selected four more supers with honey frames. Red clover meant a high volume of blooms and extra work for her miniature buzzing charges. Maybe she would need additional frames after all. About to march back out the door, she paused. "Why did you build across the road?"

"The land was for sale."

"There were at least three properties along the shoreline you could've bought. People with your money buy water views. They don't do *Little House in the Big Woods.*"

"I like the woods."

"Not good enough." She pushed past him, into the sunshine.

"What do you want from me, Addie? Blood?" Though his shoulder sagged imperceptibly, he took the supers out of her arms. Her heart twisted. He had no business helping her, and certainly not with a permanent injury. He went on, "I'll gladly give it to you if it makes you feel better. But it won't change things for us. It won't—"

She stopped. "Us? There is no us, Skip. There was *never* an us, not even when we were dating. You made that perfectly clear when you left." When he'd told her, *I need to try, Addie. I need to try and make the big leagues. Don't hold it against me.* And she hadn't. What she couldn't understand was the way he disregarded their baby. He hadn't wanted to accept the responsibility for a child he'd helped create. Even as he told her, *I'll be back for you. We'll do this together.* That's what hurt. He hadn't returned. And for that she would never forgive him.

Of course, now it was all clear.

He'd had another woman in the wings. Same old Skip.

Biting back the ache in her throat, she walked to the truck. Michaela sat on the front stoop with Felicity, the American Girl doll, against her chest.

"Want to get in the truck, puddin'?" Addie said. "We're leaving now."

Lips working to release words, the child looked to Skip.

Addie set the supers on the ground and hurried to her daughter. "What is it, button?" Had Michaela heard them arguing in the shed?

She glanced over her shoulder at the man loading the pickup's bed, his arm muscles delineated and tanned in the sunlight. Once those arms had held her. Once they had kept her safe, made her feel wanted.

God, what was she doing, mooning over Skip Dalton's muscles?

She turned to her child. "Slow and easy, angel," she whispered. "Slow… That's my girl. Nothing's going to hurt you."

Addie watched her daughter's gaze dart to the side, before she felt Skip crouch beside her. His knee brushed her calf muscle and shot heat into her blood. Keeping her smile in place, she prayed her eyes were calm. She did not want Michaela recalling any unpleasant Dempsey memories.

"Hi, Michaela," Skip said softly. "I'm Becky's daddy. Remember Becky who came over today from the house across the road?"

The child's eyes were anxious as she looked at Addie.

"Slowly, baby," she whispered. "It's okay. Skip's our new neighbor. He's… He's not here to hurt me. He came to meet us."

Beside her, Skip shifted so his position left a small gap between them. "That's right, Michaela. And when Becky gets her room all fixed up, she'll show it to you. With your mommy's permission, of course."

"I l-l-like B-B-B-Becky," came her tiny voice.

Addie swallowed hard. "I know you do, button."

"C-c-c-can s-s-s-she come over t-t-to play?"

"Maybe one day." She brushed aside her daughter's wispy bangs. "Ready to go to our bees?"

A quick head bob.

"Come on, then." Taking Michaela's hand and ensuring she stood as a buffer to Skip, Addie walked to the truck's passenger door.

When she'd buckled her daughter in place, she went around back to retrieve the remaining supers, but Skip had completed the job and was slamming up the tailgate.

"How long has she been stuttering?" he asked, and instead of curiosity or repugnance, she heard a parent's gentle concern.

Her heart battled. She did not want him concerned. She did not want him to be gentle or genuine or kind. She wanted him to be the Skip Dalton she remembered. The one who chose footballs and adulation over diapers and 2:00 a.m. feedings.

Still, she considered. She could make up a story, or tell him to mind his own affairs. After all, she owed Skip Dalton zip.

On a long sigh, she decided to go with the truth. Best from her than the grapevine. "It started when she was learning to speak, but it worsened when her father walked out on us last year."

She held his gaze. *The way you did.*

One large hand rubbed the back of his neck. "I'm sorry."

Sure. She shook out her keys. "Goodbye, Skip."

He simply looked at her. Then, nodding, he said, "See you around," and headed back the way he'd come, down her narrow dirt lane to his big house winking its white walls through a lace of green wilderness.

Chapter Three

The village of Burnt Bend hadn't changed much since Skip was a kid. It was still half the size of a football field with one main drag offering island residents Dalton Foods—his family's store—a barber shop, a post office, a gas pump, a coffee shop, three restaurants, Saturday flea markets, a movie theater and Burnt Realty. If he walked a hundred feet, he'd be at the water's end of Main, and the marina where the ferry docked.

Parking his pickup in a slot near the dinky little hardware store where he'd worked when he was sixteen, Skip cut the engine. He wondered what his mother was up to in her store down on the corner. What she'd do if he walked Becky into that office above the food aisles.

He looked across the cab at his daughter in her tattered jean shorts and pink hoodie, and smiled. *Not today,* he thought. But soon. First, she needed to get acquainted with Addie. His mother would have to wait. The last thing he wanted was family overload.

"Ready to check out the mailboxes?" he asked. For Becky's sake, he wanted the *Island Weekly* delivered to his rural route address. It still surprised him that a child her age enjoyed reading the paper.

"And a birdhouse?" Her blue eyes glinted.

"And a birdhouse," he agreed as they climbed out of the truck. Truth was, there wasn't much he could refuse when it came to those Addie-eyes.

"Hey," she said. "There's Ms. Malloy and Michaela."

Skip looked across the street. Sure enough, Addie and her daughter stood on the sidewalk in front of the library, watching them.

He lifted a hand.

Towing Michaela behind her, Addie turned toward the building.

Skip pocketed his keys. Did she remember *their* rides around the island in his old Chevy pickup? The way she'd snuggled against his side, laughed in his ear?

"Michaela," Becky called.

The little girl waved before going inside.

"I'm going over to say hi."

Before Skip could stop her, Becky dashed across the pavement. "Be right back," she hollered, jogging to the library door.

Heaving a sigh, Skip jaywalked after her and told himself those four years in foster homes had initiated a fierce independence in his little girl, an independence to which he had yet to adapt.

The library had once been a military store. Low ceilings, wooden walls and floors, small windows that allowed a minimal allotment of natural light. The familiar scent of Murphy's soap, wax and books hit his nose the instant he stepped inside. The rooms hadn't changed. It was as if he'd checked out a novel yesterday, when he was eighteen and was still favored in the circle of football, Friday-night games and girls.

Except, he wasn't eighteen, he was thirty-three. And a father to an almost thirteen-year-old. A man with a shoulder that one day would likely attract arthritis.

In the children's corner he spotted Addie kneeling on the floor with Becky and Michaela. Heads bent together, both girls had several books scattered between them.

Addie's eyes lifted at his approach. "Skip."

Naturally she wouldn't make a scene with her child and Becky this close, but just the same he caught the edge she spun on his name.

"Addie." For the first time, he noticed she wore running gear: black shorts, yellow breathable shirt, yellow visor cap and a pair of gel-cushioned ASICS jogging shoes. His eyes went to the curve of her tawny ponytail; she looked Becky's age.

"Hey, Dad." Grinning, his daughter held up two small novels. "Michaela can read chapter books already. Isn't that great?"

"That's terrific, honey."

Murmuring to Michaela, Addie rose to her feet.

"We'll be fine, Ms. Malloy," Skip heard Becky respond.

Addie touched the smaller child's hair before stepping around the pair and walking to where he stood.

Her eyes—storm-blue eyes—beckoned him across the room to the fiction section. There, well out of earshot of the kids, she faced him. "Are you here to check out some books?" *Why did you follow me into the library?* her eyes asked.

"My daughter wanted to say hello to your girl," he said.

"Oh." She blinked.

"Look, Addie—"

"No, you look, Skip. I know we'll be seeing each other in town. Except for the very rich living on the water, the island hasn't changed much over the years. You probably read the stats on Burnt Bend's welcome sign."

"Population one-thousand and eight-nine?" he asked, and felt a corner of his mouth lift. "By my calculations, it's shot up a count of eighty-four since I left."

"Laugh all you want. The point is it's a small place, a small island. People know each other. They talk. Get my meaning?"

He sobered. "And you don't want them talking about us."

"As I said—"

"Yeah. I know. There is no us."

"No."

Her eyes captivated him. Once, long, long ago, he'd whispered that he could have drowned in her eyes. Clichéd, he knew. Truth was he had drowned in her soul. Until his father had yanked him out and kicked him to shore.

Skip took a deep breath. "Addie, can we call a truce? What happened thirteen years ago… We can't bring that time back, can't revert to the past." Her eyes hardened. Dammit, he was saying it all wrong. "Look, what I mean is, if I could, I'd go back. I'd change it all. You were every—"

"Excuse me. My daughter's made her choice." She stepped around him and joined Michaela and Becky at the front counter. Several minutes later, the girls said goodbye and the Malloys left.

"Dad?" Becky whispered. "What's going on?"

He pretended to study titles on the shelves. "Nothing."

"Yes, there is. Something's up between you and Ms. Malloy. I can tell." His daughter's eyes narrowed. "You *know* her, don't you? From when you lived here. Did you go to school together or something?"

Or something. He wouldn't lie. "I've known her since we were kids. But, I'd rather not talk about it right now, okay?"

"Sure. Whatever."

He exhaled a lungful of air. "It's…um, complicated, Bean."

"No worries," she said, and shrugged. "No sense crying over spilled milk. That's what Jesse always said."

Skip didn't want to discuss her adopted father. However, he admitted, "He was right. Did you choose a novel?"

She held up a copy of *Forever In Blue* and he chuckled. She loved the "traveling pants" series. Last month she'd devoured *Girls in Pants.* "Which one is that?"

"The fourth. And I'm getting this one, too." She held up a copy of *Birdhouses You Can Build In A Day.* "Then we can have baby birds every year." Her smile dazzled him.

"Fine." He selected a novel without reading the title or the author before heading for the checkout counter. "We need a couple of library cards," he told the librarian, the same woman who had ruled the books in the building during his high school days. She'd been ancient back then, too.

"Well, now," she said, her eyes sharp and keen. "Skip Dalton. Heard you were back in town."

"Yes, ma'am, Ms. Brookley." And before she could allude to something unsavory, he added, "This is my daughter, Becky."

The old woman's eyes widened. "You don't say. What grade will you start in September, Becky?"

"Seventh."

"You good in math?" The old lady typed their names onto the cards.

"Yeah. I mean, yes."

"Then you'll have no trouble with Ms. Malloy. She'll be your teacher." The librarian cast Skip a censured glance, one he read clearly: *You've got nerve coming back here with* your *kid after leaving Addie to give up hers.*

Three minutes later he filled his lungs with tangy ocean air as they walked from the musty room and the old lady's scorn into sunshine.

"Let's see what kind of mailboxes they have at the hardware store," he said, and started for the store across the street.

"Dad," Becky began, "I want to know what's up with you and Ms. Malloy. And don't say nothing. I saw the way she was looking at you."

"And how was that?"

"Like she wanted to bite your head off."

And then some. "It's a long story, Bean. One day I'll tell you, I promise."

"Why not today?"

"There are some things she and I need to work out first, okay?"

They crossed the street and walked down the sidewalk.

"Was she like your girlfriend in high school?"

Grinning, he tugged gently on her ponytail. "Persistent, aren't you? I'll tell you all in good time."

"She's a runner, you know."

"I saw that."

"She runs three times a week with her sisters. Did you know she has two sisters living here? Michaela's so lucky to have aunts."

"Michaela tell you all this?"

"Yep. And other stuff."

"Such as?"

His daughter laughed. "No way. I'll tell when you tell."

"Like I said—"

"You'll tell me when the time's right."

"Smart girl. Now, let's find us a mailbox."

"And a birdhouse?" Becky tossed a saucy look as she pushed open the door of the store, tinkling its bells.

"One birdhouse coming up."

Anything to keep questions about Addie out of his daughter's radar range. The girl was far too perceptive. *Ah, just own up, Skip. You aren't ready to disclose* that *part of your past yet.*

Nor would he contemplate the possibility that, since he'd moved within a short jog of Addie's door, his feet might be getting a tad cold.

Sweat ran down Addie's ribs and spine and between her breasts. Today she led her sisters. Usually it was Kat, then Lee, then Addie. But after seeing Skip at the library, she needed to push harder than ever. She needed to outrun the memories.

Right, and when has that ever happened? You even married a man who resembled Skip. Dark hair, honey eyes.

God, she'd made so many foolish, foolish decisions.

In a groove now, she paced herself, breathing through her mouth and lengthening her stride, yet maintaining a slower pace. Wednesday was always their long run, nine miles around Silver Lake in the middle of the island, while on Monday and Saturday they ran the ocean shoreline.

Initially, it had been Addie and her middle sister, Kat, out-running stress and grief. Lovely, dark-haired Kat, who'd lost her husband in a boating accident while Addie still had nightmares over her lost baby, never mind her problems with Dempsey.

Then their eldest sister Lee returned, lugging a heart full of baggage to the island, and running had become as necessary as water to the trio.

"So," Lee said, coming abreast with Addie. "Where's the fire?"

"No fire." She kept her eyes on the forested trail ahead.

"Yeah? At this pace we'll be finishing the lake run in twenty minutes, not our normal ninety."

Addie checked her watch as they passed the ancient sequoia. Seven minutes too fast; she slowed her pace.

Behind them, Kat asked, "This about Skip Dalton?"

"What about him?" Lee asked.

Addie said, "Kat thinks because he's moved in across the road from me I'm running to escape."

"Are you?" they asked in unison.

"No. Where he lives is not my concern. What he does is not my concern. Who he does it *with* is not my concern."

"Really?" Kat's chuckle drifted between Addie and Lee. "You seem to be mighty vocal about the whole thing for him not to be *your* concern, honey."

"Did you see him today?" Lee asked as they emerged from the woods and started down the path along the lakeshore. "Is that why you're upset?"

"I'm not upset."

At least not anymore.

Not since they'd begun their run. In the library she believed Skip had deliberately tracked her down, but then Michaela told Addie on the way to Charmaine's house that Becky had wanted to say hi and get a library card.

Addie couldn't fault the girl. She was polite and kind, and Michaela liked her. A lot. Which scared Addie. Her daughter hooking up with Becky meant Skip and Addie were doomed to each other's company.

Beneath her feet the ground was spongy, the track easy; in her lungs the air was fragrant with pine and moss and lake water. She had trekked this trail with Skip when she was fifteen. He had kissed her here when she was sixteen, and around the next bend seven months later he had made love to her for the first time under a soft August moon, in the back of his pickup.

"*I wish it was a bed,*" he'd whispered. And she'd whispered in return, "*I'm glad it's just you and me and the moon.*"

Silly romantic fool, that's what she'd been.

"Addie?" Lee's voice plunged her back to the present. "'Fess up. What gives? You've been a bear with a sore paw for more than a week."

"Fine." Before they made the bend and The Spot, she slammed to a halt. "Here's the deal. I'm scared."

Lee yanked the bandana from her thick, curly red ponytail, and wiped her neck. "Of Skip?"

"Yes, of Skip."

Kat, always the hugger, put her arms around Addie. "Honey, why on earth would you be scared of him?"

Lee rolled her eyes. "Not of him, of herself."

"Is that it?" her middle sister asked.

Addie nodded. "He's right across the road. I'll not only see him at school, but I'll see him when I'm home. I'll see his car in his driveway…or him doing something in his yard—building mailboxes and birdhouses—"

"Birdhouses?" her sisters parroted.

"Becky told Michaela they were getting a birdhouse today."

"Why is that scary?" Kat wanted to know.

"I don't know." Hands on her hips, Addie hung her head and blew out a breath. "Because it's homey. It means they're staying."

"But you already knew that, Addie." As eldest, Lee had learned early to be the logical one. "You knew when he took on Coach's job."

Both sisters studied her.

"You still have feelings for him," Lee observed.

"Not at all."

"Oh, Addie." Kat, the peacekeeper, the nurturer.

Backing away, Addie held up her palms. "Don't start with the 'Oh, Addie.' I'm over him, all right? I haven't thought of Skip Dalton in years." She turned to run the trail again.

"Sheesh, you're just like Mom," Kat called after her.

"Mom's got nothing to do with this," Addie retorted.

"Yes, she does." Lee was on her heels. "You won't own up."

Own up. The way Charmaine wouldn't own up about Kat's father. "This is hardly the same," Addie said. "I know who Skip Dalton is."

"But," Lee said, "you've never accepted your feelings where he's concerned. You've shoved them into the back closet. Just like Mom."

Just like Mom. *No way.* Addie ran toward the trail's bend, the bend where he'd told her he loved her, that he would never leave her, that one day they'd be two old people rocking on the porch, watching sunsets. And when she reached the curve, when she might have stumbled, she ran harder, faster, escaping what she believed buried for thirteen years….

That Lee was right.

* * *

Standing on her back stoop, Addie called for Michaela. No response. She hurried to the honey house in case her daughter had gone there. The child liked sitting on the wooden floor in a sunny spot playing with her dolls, and Addie suspected it had to do with the waxy-honey scent and quiet warmth. "Michaela!"

The door was closed.

Worry spiking, she rushed inside the building. Empty.

Where was she?

Running to the front yard, she called again. Then stopped when the sound of hammering echoed through the late-morning air.

Hadn't he finished building over there yet?

And suddenly she knew where her daughter had gone. *The birdhouse.*

The one Becky described to Michaela last night on the phone—already they'd exchanged numbers. The one the girl had convinced Skip to buy following the library trip two days ago and their discussion about tree swallows nesting in Addie's backyard.

Quickly, she walked down the path shaded by evergreens and birch, and across the road. At the end of his driveway, a spanking white mailbox stood on a clean-cut wooden post. The mailbox he'd purchased while she jogged with Lee and Kat.

Across each metal side the name DALTON had been stenciled in black block lettering, and for a second, she couldn't breathe.

A strong name for a headstrong man.

He'd always done what he wanted, what he deemed necessary for his profession. Once, she had loved his name. Written it a hundred times in her school notebooks and carved it into a tree along with her own in the woods behind her mother's house.

A.W. + S.D. enclosed in a heart.

Stupid. A stupid girl with silly dreams and impractical hopes.

Today, she was a woman of independence, living under the rule of pragmatism and common sense—she hoped—and Skip Dalton had neither.

She walked down his graveled drive, her mind on retrieving her daughter, whose giggles erupted from behind the white-and-green house.

Michaela and Becky were attempting cartwheels on a grassy patch several yards from the wide-lipped back porch, while Skip read the instructions to what appeared to be the celebrated bird-house. Pieces of cardboard lay scattered on a stone walkway in front of the porch stairs.

Addie stared. The scene appeared almost ruthless. Skip the family man—a father with two girls—working in the yard, fixing things. All they needed was a dog lying in the sun, thumping its tail.

And a woman—

Addie refused to let the thought gel. Refused to think of the woman connected to Skip through his child. Refused to wonder who and why—

"Mommy!" Spying her, Michaela ran forward. "Me 'n' Becky can do cartwheels!" She grasped Addie's hand. "Come watch, Mommy."

At her child's shouts Skip turned his head and his dark gaze streaked through her like a hot wind. She remained where she stood. "It's time to go home, button. We have to check the bees."

Michaela shook her head, her lips working her thoughts. "B-b-but I want to s-s-stay with B-B-Becky."

"It's all right, Ms. Malloy." Becky walked over. "Mick can stay with us until you get back. Can't she, Dad?"

"Absolutely," he agreed. "She's welcome anytime."

Mick. Hadn't she told the girl a week ago Michaela hated the nickname? Dempsey used to call her Sticky Micky when she stuttered. Except today, her daughter seemed at ease and happy with the butchered version.

"Please, Mommy. I wanna s-s-stay with them. I wanna do m-m-more c-c-cartwheels. B-B-Becky's t-t-teaching me."

"Michaela." Addie knelt on the grass in front of her child. "You can come back another time, okay?"

Her daughter's bottom lip poked out. She shook her head, swinging her long dark pigtails. Tears plumped in her brown eyes and clung to her lashes.

"P-p-please, Mommy," she whispered. Her little arms wrapped Addie's neck. "Becky's my f-f-friend."

Oh, God. How could she refuse? This preteen, this *child of Skip's,* had offered something Michaela sorely lacked: camaraderie.

He walked over to where Addie knelt with Michaela in her lap.

"She'll be safe with us, Addie." His deep voice seeped into her pores. "Count on it."

Count on it. The way she'd been able to count on him when he'd said, *This was not my choice.*

"I'm not counting on anything."

Rising to her feet, she hoped her eyes conveyed exactly what she meant. She hadn't depended on a man in a long, long while. She wasn't about to start now. And definitely not with Skip Dalton.

"I understand," he said, and she saw he'd connected the dots.

Becky interjected, "So can Mick stay, Ms. Malloy?"

"*Please,* Mommy." Michaela leaned against Addie, tear-streaked face upturned.

Becky's my friend. "Honeykins, I…" *Would rather you find someone else.* But who? Last year, some of the first-grade kids had teased her about stuttering. Becky was different. Kind and sweet and genuine. "All right."

"Goody!" Michaela rushed to her newfound pal and grabbed her hand. "I get to stay, B-B-Becky."

"Yep. Want to go in and get a Popsicle?"

"Mom," Michaela yelled. "I get to have a P-P-Popsicle!"

"I heard, love. Only one, okay?"

"Uh-huh, or my tummy g-g-gets sick." She skipped at Becky's side as the pair went up the deck steps and into the house.

Addie glanced at Skip. "Do you have a pen? You'll need my cell number in case something happens."

"Nothing's going to happen. The girls will be right here with me."

She hoped her look was direct. "It'll make me feel better if you had my number." She frowned at the sound of "my number," and added, "For safety reasons."

"Fine." He removed a small notebook and carpenter's pencil from his hip pocket. Among ciphers and construction sketches, he wrote in his left-handed script, Addie-Cell and the number she recited.

"Thank you." She turned toward the lane. "I won't be long."

"Addie." Massaging his left shoulder, he walked with her around the side of his house. "It's good the kids get along, don't you think?"

She continued down his driveway. "It doesn't mean we'll be friends, Skip, so don't read anything into it."

"I'm not. I just wish…"

Halting midstride, she gazed up at him—at those honey eyes, that two-day beard, the too-long hair edging out from under his ballcap. "What? That we'll be friends? That the past didn't exist and I didn't hate you for what you said and did?"

She saw him swallow before he looked away and wished she could recall her words. She hadn't meant for him to know her grief, her hurt. And if she were honest with herself, neither had she meant to hurt him.

She resumed her mission, bent on her house, truck and bees. An hour and she'd return for Michaela, to have a chat with her daughter about crossing roads and going to the neighbor's house without permission.

Michaela had to understand the gravity of her actions, of stranger-danger. One day her life could depend on it.

"Addie." She heard his voice through a haze of worry and frustration.

With a sigh, she turned. He stood twenty feet up the driveway.

"Bee sting," he said softly.

Bee sting. His code when they were teenagers, whenever she fought with her father and cried over his strict regimen, his harsh and opinionated philosophy. The words had helped her put things into perspective. Bee stings were ultimately worse than arguing with a parent.

As she gazed at Skip, she understood. Having him as her neighbor or having their children like each other was not as bad as an allergic reaction that squeezed air from windpipes— his windpipe.

Clamping her bottom lip at *that* memory, she turned for home, grateful he'd been a survivor that day. Because no matter what she believed about the past, nothing compared to seeing a twelve-year-old boy writhing on the ground, fighting for his next breath.

Chapter Four

What do you wish? That I didn't hate you for what you said and did?

Addie's words were a battering ram on his heart as he watched her walk away. He knew what she was talking about; knew the time and place—that day in the rain—and he heard the words that were said, all over again….

He had gone to pick her up to take her to dinner, to the movie *Seven*. But from the moment she climbed into his old Chevy, she'd been quiet, not ecstatic, and hadn't recognized the energy radiating off his body. She'd always been in tune to him. But not that night. That night she had slipped into the seat, buckled up and kept her face averted.

"Hey, honey. I missed you today."

He'd tried to kiss her before starting the car and felt the change in her then, but he shrugged it off, too high with his own euphoria. The call from the NFL scout had come an hour before.

Her subtle withdrawal probably meant she'd had another

fight with Cyril, which Skip didn't want to discuss. Not when he was damn near jumping out of his skin with excitement. He wanted to take her to a place for a nice meal to tell her, then to celebrate he wanted to park in their favorite spot along the lake and make love with her.

"Where would you like to eat?" he asked, driving away from her house. Rain smudged the windshield and he turned on the wipers. He glanced across the seat; she stared out the side window into the darkness. "Addie?"

Her walnut-colored hair swung along her shoulders as she shook her head. "I don't want to eat. I'm not hungry."

"Something wrong?" A small alarm bell rang when she remained silent. "You mad at me?"

"No," she said, and he thought she murmured, *I'm mad at myself,* but he wasn't sure because the radio was playing the oldies station she loved.

"Then where?" He was starving, but he'd grab a burger if she didn't want to do the dinner scene.

"I don't care."

A streak of annoyance touched Skip. This was his big night. Couldn't she sense his excitement?

He turned the wipers on high—like his inner alert signal. When he pulled into a burger joint, it was packed with people they'd known forever. Teenagers and college kids home for spring break. Skip killed the ignition and they listened to the rain drum on the hood.

And then she said the words, the ones that changed both their lives. "I'm late, Skip."

Late. Oh, yeah. He knew exactly which *late* she meant.

Staring through the windshield he could see his life falling...falling into an abyss. His heart pounded, his palms grew clammy. "You sure?"

Still, she hadn't looked at him, but stared instead through the rain-blurred glass. "I took the drugstore test this morning. Twice."

No mistake. They'd made a baby, that's what they'd done. Using condoms worked, but sometimes, *sometimes* things happened. Sometimes they broke, and sometimes they were forfeited for the real thing. Which they'd done once. *Once—*

He set his forehead on the steering wheel, tried to swallow while his mind spun with futuristic scenarios.

A cramped, dingy apartment. Construction work. Bills. Creditors.

"I'm keeping it," she whispered, and he lifted his head. "You don't need to stick around." For the first time she looked at him. "I won't ruin your plans."

In the darkness of night and rain, relief whirled through him, before shame settled and he took up her cold wringing hands. "Addie, we'll work this out."

"How?" The word was so full of hope he wanted to cry.

"I don't know, but we will. I promise." He pulled her into his arms, kissed her forehead. "It'll be all right, honey. We'll be okay." He meant every word. The baby was his and he would *be* its daddy in a different way than his own father had been to him.

Three weeks later in the same spot, the same car, he'd told her, "This wasn't my choice" and she'd leapt out and slammed the door before he could explain the power a father had over his son.

Before he could admit his own weakness.

The next day he'd left Firewood Island forever.

Becky was curious about Ms. Malloy's bees. Michaela had told her a little about how the bees were kept in hives and how when Ms. Malloy brought home the frames—whatever they were—she spun them around to get the honey out. The whole process fascinated Becky. She knew Ms. Malloy checked the hives twice a week and today—Wednesday—was one of those days.

She knocked on the front door. The sun hid behind a collection of gray clouds and she could smell rain in the air.

"Hi," Becky said with a smile when Ms. Malloy opened the door. "I was wondering if you wanted some help with your bees today."

The woman's eyebrows rose and she peered past Becky. "Where's your father?"

"In town getting groceries. We're barbecuing chicken tonight." Then on a rush she said, "You and Michaela can come over and eat with us."

"I don't think—"

"Oh, Mommy, say yes!" Michaela's feet thundered from somewhere inside the house before she flung herself around her mom's waist. "Hi, Becky!"

"Hey, Mick. What you got there?"

"My new B-B-Barbie. Wanna see?"

Respectfully, Becky said, "May I come in, Ms. Malloy?"

The woman hesitated. "Does your dad know you're here?"

"I left him a note." She didn't say the note mentioned she hoped to see the beehives. She wouldn't deceive her dad, but she also hoped she'd be out in the fields or back home before he returned so he couldn't do anything about her adventure. He hadn't told her *not* to be around beehives, just that he was severely allergic to the insect's stinger. Which translated to "this is serious and don't take the chance."

But Becky had taken a lot of chances in her life. Working around beehives would be easy.

Michaela danced on her toes. "Mom, can Becky come in and see my room first?"

Ms. Malloy stepped aside. "Just for a minute. We have to check the hives before it rains."

Becky grabbed her chance. "Could I come along? I really wanna see how you get the honey and stuff." She gave the woman a huge grin.

"Well…" Ms. Malloy rolled her lips inward. "Your father is—"

"I'll sit in the truck," Becky offered. "I won't interfere. And don't worry. I'm not allergic."

"Mom, I want Becky to come." Michaela tugged on her hand. "She's my friend. *Please*. Can't we show her the bees?"

"All right." Ms. Malloy glanced out the door once more— probably imagining Becky's dad charging down the road. "Two minutes, then we leave."

The Malloy house was old, but kind of neat. Becky peeked in the front room, kitchen and bathroom. She didn't go near Ms. Malloy's room.

Michaela's room faced a wooded backyard, like Becky's room in the new house. Becky liked it immediately, the way it was all pink and white. Her old bedroom—the one she'd slept in when her mom was still alive and her dad wasn't in jail—had walls covered in dark, fake-wood panels and the floor had been linoleum. Her dresser had been bought at a garage sale and her mom had painted it white so it looked like a bright splash in a dull room.

Michaela's Barbies were lined up along a shelf above a pink-and-white dresser. The little girl chattered like one of those excited squirrels in the trees at her dad's house. Not once did she stutter and Becky wondered if her mother working in the kitchen heard the difference. A few minutes later, Ms. Malloy called, "Time to go."

Michaela tucked a doll against her chest. "Mom lets me take a Barbie. This'll be Princess's second trip." She caught Becky's fingers. "Come on."

Outside, they loaded the truck with frames for the bees' honeycombs. They drove to a red clover field first. There Ms. Malloy and Michaela dressed in white coveralls, gloves, boots and wide-brimmed hats with nets wrapping around their faces and necks.

"Why white?" Becky wanted to know, watching the pair climb into the suits.

"Because it's invis'ble," Mick piped up. "Right, Mom?"

"Really?" Becky hadn't known that.

"When you disturb the hive," Ms. Malloy said, "the bees look for something to sting. Dark clothing attracts them— white hides us."

"Wow." When she was little she would've given anything to *hide* when her parents argued and her dad got mean. A white suit wouldn't have worked, but as a kid Michaela's age, Becky might have believed it.

Ms. Malloy lit the smoker, then gave it to Mick to carry while she took a stack of frames to the first hive.

Over the next half hour, Becky watched Mick's mother calm the bees with the smoker, and work around the hives. Some honey-filled frames they loaded in the truck, some they left as winter food for the hive.

"So you won't be collecting any more honey?" Becky asked.

Ms. M. tossed the bee suits in the truck bed. "The honey season is almost over. In September the bees prepare for winter."

"Oh." Becky hid her disappointment. Now she'd have to wait 'til next summer before putting on a suit and really helping. But maybe that was good, too. By next summer she hoped Ms. M. would like her enough to let her be a sort of assistant.

They all climbed into the truck to drive to the cucumber patch and the second set of hives.

Suddenly a car approached. Becky recognized the silver Prius. "Uh-oh. That's my dad."

He didn't turn into the field's access lane, but stopped on the main road. From where she sat she could see by his expression she'd done wrong. Something really wrong.

"Your note explained about the bees, right?" Ms. Malloy asked.

"I thought we'd be back before he got home."

"Oh, Becky." Ms. M. sighed.

Shame churned Becky's stomach. *This* dad was a good man.

Not only had he saved her from foster care, but he'd given her a life she'd never experienced or expected. Most of all, he loved her the way a father should love his daughter—with kindness. She shouldn't have tricked him.

Ms. Malloy got out of the truck.

Eyes big, Michaela hugged her Barbie close. "Is your d-d-dad m-m-mad?"

"No, Mick. But I should talk to him. You going to be okay for a minute?"

The little girl nodded. "D-d-don't let h-h-him hurt you, B-B-Becky."

Upon impulse, Becky hugged the child. "My daddy's a nice guy, Mick. He loves me."

"M-m-y d-d-daddy d-d-didn't l-l-love m-m-me."

Becky's heart gave a lurch. *Just like Jesse,* she thought. "We'll talk later, 'kay?"

"'Kay."

Becky followed Ms. Malloy to the Prius.

Her dad rolled down the window a few inches. "You okay?" he asked, worry plain in his tone.

"I'm fine, Dad. I'm sorry. I should've called your cell instead of leaving a note."

The EpiPen he wore on his belt at all times lay on the passenger seat. Her dad stared at the cluster of hives. From here, they looked like little white Lego blocks against the dark clover field. Again shame swept through Becky. How could she have forgotten? She knew why he'd screened the porch. Why he'd built three *extra* birdhouses to attract swallows. Hadn't she read that flying bugs were the birds' main diet?

"Skip." Ms. Malloy stood beside Becky. "Your daughter came to keep Michaela company. She stayed in the truck with the windows rolled up while we worked the hives." And then Ms. Malloy reached toward the gap in the window and her dad's gaze went to her hand, then her face, and Becky sensed an odd current arcing between them before Ms. Malloy stepped back. "You need to go home with your father, Becky."

"Can I say goodbye to Michaela?" she asked.

When her dad nodded, she sprinted down the field lane to the truck. "Mick, get your mom to say yes about coming to supper tonight, okay?"

"Were you b-b-bad?"

"Nope," she said—like it was no big deal. She didn't want Mick worrying. "See ya later."

As she passed Ms. Malloy walking back to the truck, the woman said, "Try to remember what this means for your daddy, Becky."

"Yes, ma'am. Bees are bad for him. I need to be more careful."

Ms. M. hesitated, a puzzled look in her eyes. "Yes," she said finally. "You do."

The drive home was silent—proof that Becky had disappointed her dad. A first in the ten months they'd been a family. She was so ashamed.

Skip worried that he'd come down too hard on his daughter. But, God, he had been half out of his mind, thinking of her among those beehives.

Addie wouldn't have let anything happen. You overreacted.

And he had, and now Becky was holed up in her room, a first in many months. The moment they'd entered the house, she'd run up the stairs and hadn't come down again, though he tried twice to talk to her through the door…and received no response.

Downstairs he observed the rain approach, a dull dark bank of blue sweeping in from the Pacific Ocean, leaching light from the day. Restless, he began preparing black-forest ham sandwiches and carried them up to Becky's room.

"Bean?" he called at the closed door. "I made lunch."

"Not hungry," came her muffled reply.

"All right. But can we talk?"

Silence.

"Okay, forget talking. I'd really like some company while I eat my sandwich," he cajoled.

When he thought she'd ignore him again, the door cracked open. She wouldn't look at him, though her gaze went to the plate of food.

"Hey," he said softly.

Leaving the door, she turned and walked back to her bed, climbed up and sat against the wall, arms around her knees. Easing himself into the chair at her desk, Skip set the plate down. His heart pounded in his throat, but he took the first bite anyway. When he finally swallowed, he said, "Not bad, if I say so myself."

Becky eyed the plate, which he nudged in her direction.

She said, "I'm sorry for making you worry."

"And I'm sorry for coming unglued."

Her eyes widened. "You didn't. Not like—"

Jesse Farmer. Skip didn't want to think what her adopted father might have done.

Chin on her knees, Becky said, "I like that you worry."

"You do?"

"Yeah," she said. "It makes me feel like you care."

"I do care, Bean. More than I can describe. I want to protect you and give you everything I can."

She stared ahead. "You already have."

No, he thought. *Not everything.* But one day soon he would. One day soon, he'd give her Addie.

Breathing with relief, he nodded to the sandwiches. "Sure you don't want one?"

Her blue eyes took in the minifeast. "They got mayo?"

"Not a speck."

At that she glanced up. "You know I hate mayo?"

He couldn't stop the slow, half smile. "I hate it, too."

"Really?" She bounded to the foot of the bed and reached for the plate. "Guess I'm like you then."

"Guess you are," he replied, and his heart tumbled.

They ate in silence for a minute.

"Dad?"

"Yeah?"

"Does this mean I'm really your daughter?"

"You always were, Becks." He had explained the DNA testing before she had come to live with him, before he'd proceeded with her legal adoption from the state.

"But I always wondered where I got some habits from, y'know? Jesse used to say I got my finger-tapping from him, so I stopped doing that. I didn't want to be like him."

"Just be your own person, Becky."

"But I like having some of your ways. It makes me feel like I've got a past I can finally figure out."

A past to figure out. As a parent, he was having enough trouble figuring out *right now.* "Let's take it a day at a time." At least tomorrow was a past not yet written. And it held Addie. He could learn from her.

If she let him.

By 4:30 p.m., a deluge fell from the sky. Rain pounded the earth, creating puddles wherever there was a dip, and the wind roughhoused with the trees.

With Michaela trotting at her side, Addie hurried to the house from the honey shed, where she'd spent the afternoon scraping wax off the filled frames before extracting honey from their cells.

By mid-September the season would be over. She hoped selling almost 400 pounds of honey and dozens of candles from the wax would add a nice sum to her savings and repair the shingles lifting on her roof.

"Can we go eat at Becky's house, Mom?" Michaela asked as

they entered the kitchen through the back door. "She said her dad's barb'cuing."

Shaking back her damp hair, Addie pulled wet strands from Michaela's cheeks. "I doubt they'll be barbecuing in this weather, button." *A blessing in disguise, considering.*

"When then?"

"I don't know." *Never.*

Michaela set her doll on the table and walked to the tea towel hanging on a cupboard handle. "Don't you like M-M-Mr. D-D-Dalton?"

"I like him." *He's different now. A man with a child. And I still get flushed when I see him.*

Today she had reached out to touch him. Lord, her sisters were right. Her feelings for him were piled high and deep in the closet of her heart, and they were beginning to spill free.

Mentally liberating herself of his hold, she rolled her shoulders and went to the sink to wash her hands before starting supper.

"Was h-h-he mad at Becky 'cause she came with us?" Michaela asked, wiping rain from the doll's face.

"He was worried about her, button."

"He looked really m-m-mad."

"He wasn't." *Not every man is like your father,* Addie wanted to point out, but she knew the words would make little difference. Dempsey's dour moods had left an indelible imprint on Michaela in the few short years they had been a family.

Michaela fixed Barbie's dress. "He yelled at Becky."

Addie came to the table, sat on the chair beside her child. "Michaela, listen to me. Mr. Dalton wasn't yelling. He was very worried about Becky. See, he's allergic to bees and gets very, very sick if he's stung. So sick he can die if he doesn't get medication right away."

Michaela's eyes rounded. "C-c-can Becky d-d-die?"

"No, Becky doesn't have the same problem." *Thank God.*

"Then why d-d-does Mr. Dalton g-g-get worried?"

"She's his daughter. Everything concerning her worries him." Addie touched her child's cheek. "Just like I worry about you."

Michaela raised her head. "'Cause I s-s-stutter?"

"Oh, love." Addie brought the child around and lifted her onto her lap. "Your stuttering is just a little part of you." She snuggled Michaela close. "I'll tell you a secret. It's a parent's job to worry about their children. They want to make sure their babies are safe and happy and loved. And that never stops, even when the babies grow up."

"How c-c-come Daddy d-d-doesn't w-w-worry about me?"

"He does. In his own way." *Damn you, Dempsey, for doing this to your daughter. You could at least phone once in a while.*

Michaela was silent for a long moment. "I'm sorta s-s-scared of Mr. D-D-Dalton."

The words should not have come as a shock, but hitting Addie in Michaela's soft, tiny voice, they did. "Don't be," she murmured.

"What if he runs away from Becky? Like Daddy ran away from me?"

"Daddy didn't run away, Michaela. He *chose* to leave. He wanted to live a different life and so he left. It had nothing to do with you. *Nothing.*"

Michaela popped a thumb into her mouth, signaling that no matter what Addie said to the contrary her daughter would believe what she wanted to believe. She kissed her child's hair. She would do what *she* had to do. "No more thumb. All right?"

A small nod. The thumb reluctantly left Michaela's mouth.

Another kiss and she set the child on her feet. "Good girl. Bring over the phone and Becky's number."

Michaela's eyes rounded. "Are we eating barb'cue at Becky's?"

If the invitation still existed. "Let's see if Mr. Dalton agrees."

Michaela dashed to the counter where the notebook page lay with Skip's number in bold black beside the telephone—the page he had exchanged with her the day he'd constructed the birdhouse.

"This doesn't mean we'll be going," she said when her daughter grabbed the paper and receiver.

"But Becky said," Michaela persisted.

"It's not Becky doing the cooking, honeybun. Now, go find some dry clothes, okay?"

Michaela dashed off and Addie dialed.

"H'lo."

"It's Addie," she said, and suddenly lost her voice at the sound of his.

"Hey." Warmth and gladness encompassed the word; her heart jumped a bit. For a second, she was a teenager again, hearing that welcome and familiar baritone greeting.

She squared her shoulders. This was for Michaela. "Sorry to intrude, but Becky asked my daughter to your house for—"

"Barbecued chicken. I know." He chuckled. "Might as well get used to it, Addie. Our girls like each other—and you and I have been inadvertently tossed into the mix."

"Only as parents," she said. "Nothing more."

"Hmm." She could hear his smile. "Can you be here by five? The kids can play for a bit and we can talk while I cook."

"The hi-honey-how's-your-day kind?" she tried to tease in return, and it felt good.

He didn't hesitate. "Might as well begin somewhere. See you in twenty." Then the phone hummed.

No, she thought, *we don't have to begin at all.*

Suddenly she was exhausted. Outside the wind soughed in the trees and rain pelted the roof and washed the windows. All she wanted was to make a quick, easy meal, take a hot bath and spend the evening with a book. She did not want to go back into the storm. *Oh, face it. It's Skip you don't want to see again.*

Liar.

When the phone shrilled, she snatched it to her ear.

"I'll pick you up," he said without preamble.

"That's not necessary. I have an umbrella."

But he'd already hung up. She stared at the phone, too tired to redial and argue. Pulling herself out of the chair, she went down the hall. At Michaela's door, she asked, "Almost ready, pumpkin?"

"Uh-huh." Addie saw that her daughter had changed into a pink long-sleeved top with a sparkly Tinkerbell on the front, and pink pants. Her pink sneakers were on the wrong feet again. "I'm bringing these Barbies." Ten dolls lined her bed.

"Honey, why not bring four, instead?" Becky had been sweet about the dolls that first day, would she be again? Something told Addie yes. The girl was a kind soul. Was she like her mother, the woman Skip'd had a relationship with? "Two for you, two for Becky," Addie said, veering from the thought. "That way they won't get crowded in your knapsack."

Michaela considered. "Okay."

If only her life was as simple, Addie thought.

"Are we going now?"

"Soon as I shower. Meantime—" she pointed to the pink sneakers and whispered "—you might want to switch your shoes."

Twenty minutes later, Skip stood on the front stoop holding a huge navy-colored umbrella. Addie caught her breath at the sight of his smiling eyes, and *him* in bootcut jeans with a crease down the leg—who ironed denim these days?—and a burgundy jacket.

Rain drummed the earth and sluiced over the eaves of her roof. The wind harassed the three big hemlocks fronting her house. She barely heard the sounds because with one arm Skip had scooped up Michaela. "Come on, tyke. Let's get you into the car."

Circling Addie with the other arm, he ushered her across the gravel to his Prius, then gently stowed Michaela into the rear.

Seconds later, he'd tossed the umbrella in the trunk and climbed behind the wheel. "I've forgotten our island storms." He furrowed strong fingers into his rain-dewed hair.

Addie couldn't speak. Not once had her ex taken as much care with his family as Skip had in these few minutes. Dempsey had been about Dempsey. Becoming a father hadn't changed that trait. Oh, he loved her—when it was convenient and fit his mood—but *being* a daddy constricted his vision, his grand plan of things. Which meant, Addie realized soon enough, that Dempsey loved the *idea* of fatherhood. Not the reality of diaper changes, nor the middle-of-the-night crying and teething fusses, not the spills, messes, colds and earaches, nor the million fundamentals that raising a child set in motion from the moment of birth.

Exactly, if she analyzed it, like Skip. Yet, somewhere in the last decade he had learned to care.

Turning the ignition, he shot her a glance. A raindrop trailed along his temple. "What?" he asked, when she couldn't look away.

"You've changed."

He huffed a breath. "God, I hope so."

She faced the windshield. The wipers swathed the rain as he headed down her narrow road where evergreens and oaks swayed ominously with the wind. "Maybe," she said, "I've jumped to conclusions too fast—"

A thunderous *boom* resonated through the car.

"Jesus!" Skip slammed the brakes. Addie's heart stopped. Flinging the door open, Skip leapt out.

"Mom*my!*"

Pulse erratic, Addie tried to see through the watery rear window.

"It's all right, baby," she soothed, touching her daughter's knee as the child grabbed her hands. "Mom won't let anything hurt us." God, what had happened? Fear whipped her belly. Where had Skip gone?

"D-d-don't g-g-go, M-M-Mommy."

"I'm here, honey. I'm here." She had to rely on Skip. For the first time she had to rely on the man who had once left her in a crisis.

Please, don't let it be bad.

But she sensed the ominous. She sensed it before he bent into the open door moments later. "Addie." Rain peppered his shoulders, his hair, carved rivulets down his strong, lean cheeks. Yet all she focused on was the unhappiness in his dark eyes. "A tree's smashed your truck and house."

Chapter Five

She gazed at the destruction of her pickup and left wall of her house.

The tree was a hundred-feet tall and had been in the ground to the left of the front stoop since before her grandfather's day. What worried Addie were the remaining hemlocks swinging like a pair of trapezes in the wind and the mammoth hole hewed by the downed tree's root ball.

Addie couldn't move from the spot where she'd bumped to a stop after leaping from the car. She could see Skip's dark head and flashes of his burgundy jacket while he walked along the tree's periphery and investigated the damage. Branches covered the stoop and engulfed the truck as if it were a maroon egg shielded by a monstrous green bird.

"Mommy!"

Michaela stood beside the car, clutching a Barbie and scanning the scene with round, terrified eyes.

"Go back inside the car, honey," Addie called, wanting desperately to view the destruction more closely, but hearing her daughter's angst. "I'll be right there. Get out of the rain."

"I'm s-s-scared!" The child's gaze darted up at the trees swaying wildly along the edges of the lane.

"Skip!"

His head popped up through the branches of the downed tree.

Addie cupped her mouth. "I'm taking Michaela to your house to stay with Becky." *Where she'll be safe.* "Be back in a few minutes."

A wave and then he disappeared again.

Addie ran to the Prius. The keys were still in the ignition. Slipping behind the wheel, she started the motor...and recognized she sat where he had minutes ago, that her hands gripped the wheel where his had rested, but all thought of Skip vanished when she saw her house in the side-view mirror. Tears smarted. Her home. Her lovely, quaint little carriage house...

Wrecked in approximately three seconds.

She should have had those trees thinned last summer. Living on the island, she knew what storms could do, how they could ravage beach property, flood basements, down trees in a heartbeat onto homes and vehicles. She'd seen it a dozen times over the years.

And she'd heard the old-timers talk about thinning evergreen branches so the wind could stream through.

But what had *she* done? Left *her* trees because she hadn't been able to afford five hundred dollars to have a guy climb the trunks and chop off some of the boughs. Today they had acted as sails, blocking the wind, forcing stress on the surface roots.

And then hit her house. The trees had crushed the wall of the laundry room where, a half hour before, Michaela had thrown her wet clothes.

A knot formed in Addie's throat; she could barely breathe.

"Mommy?" Michaela spoke from the backseat. "Is our h-h-h-house g-g-g-gonna be ok-k-kay?"

Addie leaned into the rear seat and kissed her child's rosy mouth. "Everything's going to be fine, angel." She forced a smile she didn't feel. "I'm taking you to play with Becky for a little while. Would you like that?"

"Yeah." Michaela nodded, her ponytail bouncing. "Can we go now?"

"You bet." She put the car in gear. Behind them, she saw Skip tour the root hole. She wouldn't think about the repairs—or buying a new truck.

She could kick herself to forever and back about saving on the pruning costs last year, except she'd needed the money for Michaela's speech therapy on the mainland, until the new school therapist in Burnt Bend gained more inroads than the highly recommended doctor in Seattle.

She pulled up in front of Skip's house. "Come on, sweets," she said, unbuckling Michaela's seat belt. "Time for you to have some fun."

"Are you g-g-going to s-s-stay?"

"I need to see what the tree did to the house, honey."

They walked up the porch steps to the front door; it opened instantly.

"Hey, Mick." Becky's eyes held pure delight. To Addie, she said politely, "Hi, Ms. Malloy."

"Becky, a tree's fallen on our house and I have to help your dad sort things out. Could you please watch Michaela for me until we're done?"

The teenager's jaw dropped. "A tree fell...? No way!"

"It's a really b-b-b-big t-t-t-tree, Becky," Michaela piped up, spreading her arms. "Way b-b-bigger than this."

"Omigod!" Becky tugged Michaela into the house. "No worries, Ms. M. I'll look after Mick. You go."

"Thank you."

"Wait," Becky cried as Addie headed for the car. "Dad doesn't have a raincoat and neither do you." She flung open the front closet. "Here." She handed Addie a man's yellow slicker, then dug out a smaller one of the same color. "It's mine. Might be a bit small, but it'll help."

Grateful, Addie tugged on the coat. The sleeves were a few inches too short, but it would keep the damp weather at bay. "Thank you, again." The girl was a wonder. Leaning down, Addie kissed Michaela's nose. "Listen to Becky, okay? I'll be back soon as I can. Love you."

"Love you, M-M-Mommy."

Skip's raincoat under her arm, Addie ran for the Prius.

His hands were bruised and bleeding from yanking at the tree's massive boughs without gloves. He didn't care about his torn skin. Cuts healed. But Addie's house, her truck...

She must be devastated. Hell, it wouldn't surprise him if she went into a state of mild shock. He'd seen her face when she stood gaping at the damage. He'd heard her anguish when she'd called out to him about taking her little girl to his house.

Michaela. The kid was already stressed, he suspected, for a dozen other reasons. And now this. Oh, he knew nervous tension wasn't the root of stuttering. He'd done some Internet research after he had met the child two weeks ago. Stuttering, he'd learned, stemmed predominantly from the way a child's speech evolved, though the stress he or she encountered at the time could augment or prolong the disorder. He hated to think how the child would internalize a tree crashing on her home.

Not every kid is as resilient as Becky. Prickly needles scratching his face, Skip climbed among the tree's branches and tried not to dwell on the experiences his daughter had endured. Every time his mind waded into that mire, he wanted to haul off and slug something. Namely himself for not having the guts thirteen years ago to stand up to his old man and stand by the woman he'd loved.

Concentrating on what he had to do *now* for Addie, he lugged aside a limb thc diameter of his thigh. Another branch of equal size had gouged a hole into the side of the house. He nudged wet, fanlike offshoots out of the way and peered through the unbroken window next to where the tree speared the laundry room.

Fate, he thought, scanning the interior. Not only had the bough missed the glass, it missed the electrical box behind the room's inside door.

"Skip!" Addie's voice pierced his focus.

"Over here." He climbed through a slippery crisscross of branches.

Wearing a yellow slicker he recognized as Becky's, she walked toward him, awe and worry flitting across her features.

Let me hold you, he wanted to say. *Let me protect you the way I didn't before.*

She pushed a wet lock of hair from her cheek. "I can't believe this." Gaze riveted on the house, she handed over his slicker.

"It's not as bad as it looks, Addie. As soon as the storm ends, I can fix the hole, no problem." He tugged the slicker over his wet shirt.

"You?" Rain struck her face, spiked her lashes.

"I've been known to do a little construction work in my day."

"When?" Her eyes were skeptical, and he sensed she wasn't questioning *if* he could do the work, but that he had bothered to learn.

"When I retired from the NFL, a buddy and I renovated his cottage on Bainbridge. He showed me a few ropes."

"And now you can fix storm-damaged houses."

He understood her doubt. He hadn't been there when it counted.

"Addie, if you'd rather pay a licensed guy, okay. I figured I'd save you some money."

She brought her hands to her cheeks, blew a breath. "I don't know what to think anymore. I have to get this hole covered before more damage is done with the rain." She headed for the honey shed.

He walked beside her. The dampness rooted an ache in his

shoulder he hadn't felt in a while. "I have a tarp back at the house if you need it."

She glanced his way when he rolled his shoulder in an effort to alleviate the spasm. She said, "You should go home, get a heating pad on that spot. This weather can't be doing it any good."

"Thanks, but I'll survive." She wanted him gone. Well, that wasn't happening. "Michaela going to be okay?"

"Once we get to my mother's house, she'll be fine." The wind caught her slicker, flapped it against her lower back. "Grandma will get her making cookies. Nothing like a chocolate-chip cookie to fix a bad-hair day."

Except, this wasn't a bad-hair day. This was a fifteen-car pileup. "You can stay with us for the night." The words were out of his mouth before he could consider their impact. Addie, *sleeping* in his house.

Her eyes softened for a moment. "Thanks, Skip, but you and Becky have already done enough."

He let the topic drop; her mind wasn't on convenience, but on how she would salvage her house.

Behind the honey shed they found two four-foot squares of weathered plywood that had been leaning against the building several seasons.

"Do you have an ax?" Skip asked. The plywood wasn't enough and the tree branches had to be removed.

In the shed, she retrieved an ax and a handsaw, held them up with the first smile she'd shown since she opened her door twenty minutes before.

"Perfect." He took in her rain-wet mouth. The drizzle patted their heads, faces and shoulders. He raised his eyes to hers and for a moment nothing past or present mattered.

Wrenching her gaze away, Addie strode for the house.

Skip watched her go. What was the matter with him?

Lust. The word hit his solar plexus. *Well, hell.* Could he deny the twitch between his legs? He wanted her. *Right, dumb-ass. That'll really endear her to you now that her house is a disaster.*

Lifting the plywood onto his head, hands gripping each side, he followed her through the rain.

They worked for an hour, sawing branches, chopping off thinner limbs, clearing the ragged hole in the wall, hauling away debris. Addie found a ratty blue tarp, left over from her dad's bee operation, in a bottom drawer in the shed and they stretched the material across the hole.

They were positioning the plywood in place around the tarp when her thumb caught on a bent nail.

"Ouch!"

"What is it?" Skip dropped the ax and was at her side in two strides.

She had the thumb in her mouth.

"Let me see." Gently, he pulled the injured digit from between her lips. His eyes held hers. *Addie.*

Then rationale prevailed and he looked down at her injury. The nail had ripped the skin along the outside of her right thumb. "You need antiseptic. Do you have some in the house?"

"It's nothing." She tried to pull her hand away.

"It's bleeding like a gusher," he countered, hanging on. "Come on. Let's get you bandaged up."

Her hand cradled in his, he led her around to the back door. Inside, he flicked the lights. Nothing. "Looks as if you're without power." He toed off his sneakers. "Stay here and I'll check the electrical box."

He went through the house as if he'd been here a thousand times, when he'd never entered the dwelling in all the years he'd lived on the island. Addie's grandfather had lived here for forty years, though her mother had lived in Burnt Bend. *That* house he knew.

And all of it, Becky's history.

The breakers hadn't clicked off; a line was down somewhere.

He returned to the kitchen, where she stood at the sink and ran cold water over her thumb. "Got a candle we can light?"

She tapped a toe against a low cupboard. "In there."

Crouching, his shoulder brushing her thigh, Skip retrieved two hurricane candles; in a top cupboard, the matches. The room's warmth thawed his shoulder and he felt the sting of change. Shaking his arm to loosen the stiffness, he set the lit candles on the counter.

In a utility drawer he found antiseptic ointment, gauze and a box of bandages. "How's it feeling?" he asked over her shoulder, and smelled the rain in her hair, on her skin.

"Bleeding's stopped."

"Good." Gently, he washed her hand, then prepared the gauze and bandages. "You should get a couple stitches," he said, examining the slash on her skin as he drew a line of ointment onto the gauze.

"It'll heal fine without. Besides, I don't have time."

Skip lifted his head. The candlelight was in her eyes. "It'll leave a scar." He hated the thought of anything marring her skin.

"That's the least of my worries. Anyway, it's not as if I don't have a bunch of scars already."

Yes, he could see that. Here and there her hands were nicked from the work she'd done over the years with her bees and living on this property. Her work ethic—her willingness to get her hands dirty, so to speak—sent a jolt down to his gut. She was nothing like the women he'd dated, not here on the island as a teenager, not on the mainland as an adult. And for damn sure not as a quarterback in the NFL. All her life, Addie had been in a league of her own, one outside the crowd.

That uniqueness attracted him again, right here in her darkened kitchen with a storm howling around the house and flooding the windows.

With utmost care, he set the gauze around her thumb and secured it with two bandages.

"Thanks," she said when he finished.

"You're welcome." He cupped her wounded hand. "I'm glad I could help." A long moment passed and still he kept her hand in his. He felt the pulse in her wrist where his thumb rested. Her skin was warm and surprisingly soft for someone who toiled with heavy hive boxes and maintained several hundred thousand insects. Oh, yeah, he'd done a lot of Internet searching over the past two weeks. Beekeeping was not an easy job.

The flickering candles washed her cheeks and lips in rosy-gold and his gaze settled on the latter. *Addie,* he thought.

"Skip."

Her voice brought his eyes back to hers and he saw that neither had she been impervious to the long-buried emotions between them.

Swallowing hard, he began, "I never meant to—"

She shook her head. "Don't. Don't bring up the past. Don't apologize or whatever else you're thinking or regretting. It's too late." She drew away, her hand slipping free. "We need to get back to the kids. Go put on your shoes before I blow out the candles."

He did. And then she plunged the kitchen into darkness with a single breath.

Walking beside Skip through the driving rain to the Prius parked in front of her house, Addie tried hard not to think of him looking at her in the kitchen's warm candlelight.

Romantic fool, she thought stamping around puddles. *In the warm candlelight. Where is your head? You know what the man is like.*

Bowing her head against the wind, she lengthened her stride. She would call her mother to come for her and Michaela, get Charmaine to take them to Kat's B and B. There she planned to stay until she determined what to do about the damages, who to call.

Rain leaked down her collar and chilled her flesh. She should have been more prepared, watched the forecast on the news. If she weren't stuck for a vehicle, she'd be heading for her hives right now, making sure her bees were safe and sheltered.

A hard gust caught Addie full on, causing her to stumble sideways. Her hair swirled around her head and whipped into her eyes.

"Hang on," Skip called against the roaring wind. "We're almost there."

Slinging an arm around her shoulders, he tugged her to his side and bent his head to hers, shielding her as much as possible with his body as he guided her into the passenger seat. Seconds later, he was behind the wheel, the storm raging beyond the windows.

"We'll get you some dry clothes right away," he said, starting the car. Across the darkness, he offered a smile. "Becky's should fit."

Teeth chattering, Addie was too cold to argue.

Turning the car down the lane, Skip flicked the heating vents on high. In the glow of the headlights, the rain struck the earth in waves.

"It's supposed to last until sometime tomorrow morning," he said, crossing the main road into his driveway. "Your bees going to be okay?"

"They should be." She'd anchored the hives with bricks and stones and set them near tree groves in preparation for weather like this. "I'll need to check them first thing, though."

He pulled to the front of the house, and they dashed up the porch steps, into his house, where they stood dripping on the entrance mat.

Michaela, her dark hair dry and curling past her tiny shoulders, came around a corner, Becky on her heels. "Mommy!"

"Hi, baby." Addie shrugged out of the slicker, stepped from her wet shoes.

"Get Ms. Malloy some towels, Bean," Skip said. He draped their slickers over the newel posts of the stairs leading to the second floor, heedless of the water streaming onto the expensive oak wood. "And she'll need some clothes, too," he called after his daughter.

"Are we s-s-s-staying here, Mom?" Michaela asked, darting a look at Skip.

"No, sweets." She brushed the little girl's hair around her ears. "Mom's calling Gram for a ride and then we'll stay at Aunty Kat's."

"Why can't we stay here?" Michaela wanted to know.

"I'll drive you to your mother's." Skip wiped his hands down whiskered cheeks. "Ah, thanks, Bean." He took the fluffy green towels the girl brought, and handed one to Addie.

"Michaela can stay with us, Ms. Malloy," Becky said.

Addie tugged her cell from her belt. "Thank you, but you and your dad have already helped." She hit speed dial.

Her mother answered on the second ring. "Where are you?" Charmaine asked.

"We're at Skip Dalton's."

"Skip Dalton's?"

"The power is out at our place. But not here."

"It's like that all over. Part of the town has power, part doesn't. I have it, but Lee doesn't. She's staying at Kat's B and B for the night."

"Mom," Addie interrupted. "Can you come get us? A tree came down on the truck and put a hole in the side of the house."

"Oh, my *God!* Why didn't you say? Michaela?"

"She's fine. We're both fine."

"Addie, you'll have to stay there. Clover Road is blocked. They're saying trees are down two miles out of town and on the south end. And you know that means they won't get to them until tomorrow at the earliest. Will he let you stay in that big house of his?"

She sighed. "We'll work something out." *Even if I have to sleep in the honey shed.* "Talk to you tomorrow."

"Give my girl a kiss from her Gram. And Addie? I'll be thinking of you."

Thinking about her and Skip. Her mother never had been subtle when it came to her daughters' business. "Later, Mom." She snapped the cell phone closed.

Skip said, "Road's blocked."

Not a question, a fact he had discerned from her side of the phone call.

"We'll be okay." She motioned to Michaela. "Honeykins, get your coat. We're going home."

"Girls." Skip spoke to his daughter. "Can you give us a minute?"

"Come on, Mick." Becky took Michaela's hand. "Let's make some hot chocolate."

After they left for the kitchen, Skip turned to Addie. "You gave me some ultimatums over there." He nodded toward her place. "Now I'm giving you one. Don't let your emotions make things harder for your daughter. We have the room. Take advantage of it."

"And you know what my daughter wants."

"No. But I understand your feelings about the past."

"You know nothing of my feelings."

"Then," he said softly, "maybe it's time to get to know each other again."

Get to know him? How many years had she wished for another chance? *Face it, Addie. You could never hate him no matter how hard you tried to convince yourself otherwise.*

Suddenly she was exhausted—of the pretense, of the terrible yearning, the loneliness, the heartbreak.

"All right," she said. "A truce. For now."

He released a long, slow breath. "You won't be sorry, I promise."

"No promises, Skip. The last time you gave them, my life changed."

She walked past him toward the kitchen, where the girls giggled.

Chapter Six

Skip followed Addie to where Becky brewed milk for the hot chocolate. Michaela sat on a stool at the island, swinging her little feet, a happy grin on her face. She'd been chattering about school, but the moment he stepped into view, her mouth clamped shut and wariness stole into her eyes. To no one in particular, he said, "Ms. Malloy and Michaela are staying the night."

"Yay!" Becky turned from the stove and gave Michaela a high five.

Skip glanced at Addie. *At least the girls know a good thing,* he wanted to say. Instead, he went to the refrigerator, dug out cut meats, lettuce, tomatoes and mustard. "You girls have something to eat?"

"We had the leftover pizza," Becky told him. She poured steaming milk into two mugs and stirred. "Can we watch a video, Dad? Michaela hasn't seen *Ratatouille* yet."

Addie nodded and he agreed. "Why not," he said.

"Come on, Mick."

Child in tow, Becky left the kitchen.

A silence dropped. Skip set the ingredients on the counter while Addie, arms folded against her middle, wandered around the room, sizing it up, he suspected. For a moment, he watched. Would she notice the lack of trophies and photos from his former years? That those absences spelled a new life for him here, on Firewood Island?

He could see she was uncomfortable in his home—and with him. He wished he could change that.

Then she surprised him. "Becky's a lovely girl."

"Yeah." Arranging the food on the counter, he smiled. "She is that."

"Is she close to her mother?" Addie fluttered a hand. "Sorry, that was inappropriate. Forget I asked."

"No, it's okay." He laid out six slices of flax bread on one of two cutting boards. "I'd rather you heard it from me." He lifted his gaze. "Her mother's dead."

Dark as winter rain her eyes stayed on his. "I'm sorry. For you both."

She wandered closer. "When did she die?"

"Four years ago." He wanted to change the topic, but was at loss as how to detour without raising suspicion.

"Was it illness or an accident?" she asked softly, and he heard the compassion in her voice. For him or for Becky?

Get it out, be done with it. "She was killed."

And suddenly he was uncomfortable where the conversation could lead. He wasn't ready to disclose Becky's history. Not yet. The time needed to be right. *And when is that?* a niggling voice asked as he rinsed the tomatoes under the tap, set them on the cutting board. *There is no right time to tell someone their child's adopted mother was killed with violence.*

Realizing Addie hadn't spoken for a minute he looked to where she stood. Her eyes were devastated. "Skip, I don't know what to say." She glanced toward the hallway where the girls had disappeared, where sounds of the TV murmured from the den.

"There's nothing to say. It happened, it's done and Becky's moving on." He sliced the tomatoes, but the air thickened with her unspoken questions: *What about you? Are you moving on?* Glancing toward the doorway, he said, "I'd rather not talk about it right now—for obvious reasons."

Mostly, he didn't want to expound on the situation involving Jesse Farmer, or that for the past four years the man had sat behind the bars of Walla Walla's state penitentiary.

Skip clenched a tomato between his fingers so hard it broke apart, scattering juice and seeds and pulp across the cutting board. "Goddammit," he muttered, recognizing what he'd done, what he'd said. Addie would not understand that it was the criminal and not the tomato he cursed.

Hell. She must think him a ham-fisted dolt.

"Sorry. I've never been good at slicing tomatoes." The tiny fib landed on the pile of his omissions. For her sake, for the sake of their daughter.

Unless you tell her now.

Sweat popped from his skin. *Soon,* and the word, the time gap, had him breathing easier.

Addie came around the island. "Can I help?"

Her question caught him off guard; for a second he wasn't sure if she meant with Becky's circumstances or with the sandwich-making.

"Sure," he said, dumping the tomato mess down the garbage disposal unit. He rinsed the board, returned it to the island, handed her the knife and another tomato.

Standing side-by-side, he noticed that her hair had dried into a thick, tumbling mass. He'd always thought her hair beautiful, the way its tawny color captured the light like tiny segments of sunshine. As a teenager she'd called the color dishwater-blond. He'd disagreed then, and he disagreed now.

She said, "If someone had told me two weeks ago I'd be preparing food in your kitchen, I would've laughed in their face."

He spread mustard on the bread. "Me, too. But…"

She shot him a look. "What?"

"I thought about it. A lot." *Among other things.*

"You thought of me in your kitchen." A statement edged in skepticism.

"Is it so hard to imagine? We had a history, Addie." Since moving into this house, he'd pictured her in every room. And at night in his bedroom, on his king-size sleigh bed. Between the sheets. With him.

She laughed softly. "History. That's one way of putting it. A man with your connections must have a lot of history over the years."

"What's that supposed to mean?"

"That I don't believe you ever gave me a thought." With a chef's efficiency, the tomato slices fell like dominoes from her fingers. "Every time you were on TV you had different eye candy on your arm." She shook her head. "God, I can't believe I said that after what you just told me about your wife. Forgive me. I'm not thinking clearly at the moment."

Her cell phone chimed a Beethoven serenade and Skip let out a slow breath. He'd been saved from explaining her incorrect interpretation about Becky's mother and his "wife."

Addie pulled the phone from her belt, flipped it open, checked the caller. "Hey, Kat."

Skip watched her walk across the kitchen to the patio doors facing the backyard, where night had rolled in, a black shroud.

"Yeah," she said to her sister. "Wind blew a tree into the house. The pickup's ready for the junkyard… Hmm… Well, Mom's a worrywart." Long pause. "Uh-huh… Not going to happen… Because, it's not, that's why." Another pause. "Look, I'll talk to you tomorrow… I'd rather you didn't… Because—" she hissed, and Skip imagined Kat's topic of conversation. Him.

"It's none of anyone's business," Addie went on. "Okay, stop right there… No… Goodbye, Kat. And tell Lee I'm fine. No need to call." She released a soft snort and snapped the phone shut.

"Problems?" he asked, layering lettuce on the bread.

"Nothing I can't deal with."

Interpretation: *he* was nothing to worry about.

"It's nice to have family concerned about you." He said it mildly, and thought of his mother living alone, a mother with whom he'd been semiestranged for thirteen years. If it hadn't been for Becky, Skip would've left things the way they were and not bought this property eight months ago.

"Depends on the concern." Addie's dark eyes held a past not forgotten or forgiven: parental interference that cost them their child.

"But now it's different." He scooped the sandwiches onto two plates. "Now we're adults."

"Technically we were then, too." Taking a dish, she walked to his kitchen table. "Thank you for the sandwich. Want me to make some tea?"

In other words, subject closed. "Eat," he said. "Would you like some wine instead?"

"Tea is fine."

"I'll put on the kettle."

Beethoven's ringtone played again. Addie checked the caller. "Oh, for heaven's sake… Lee," she said into the phone, "I told Kat you didn't— Is that so? Well, just to put you at ease—" she glanced in Skip's direction "—he's being the perfect gentleman… Absolutely not. Look, I'll talk to you guys tomorrow, okay? And tell Mom to put a stopper in her mouth. She's driving me nuts with her worrying."

Again the phone clicked shut.

"Seems you have a cavalry ready to gallop to your rescue," he teased.

"Sometimes being the youngest is truly a PITA."

"A PITA?"

"Pain in the ass."

Skip chortled with an ease he hadn't felt in years. "Eat up, Ads. Then I'll show you your room."

"The couch will do."

"Probably, but this is a big house with several bedrooms. As a matter of fact, you can sleep in mine."

She barked a laugh. "You're kidding, right?"

"I meant alone. Though I'm flattered you'd assume I'd want us to share it together."

"You know the definition of assume, right?"

"All too well." He joined her at the table, lifted his sandwich in a toast. "Here's to you and me." With a wink, he took a bite.

"Did you forget?" she asked around an ephemeral smile. "There is no you and me."

Yes, she'd told him. Twice. Or was it three times?

Truth was the secret he carried could seal the *no us* deal forever—or it could swing them in a positive direction, one that made them a family.

Both options quivered through his body.

Addie stared at the sleigh bed, expansive as a field of clover with its medley of russets and greens and yellows. Bold colors that warmed the room at once and had her trembling where she stood.

Skip's bed.

He hadn't been joking with that *you can sleep in mine*.

Leading her upstairs, he'd explained his lack of furniture on the second floor, the lack of beds for the guest rooms, something he needed to amend before too long because, once school began in a couple of weeks, Becky would want sleepovers with her new girlfriends.

"Sheets are fresh," he said, leaning in the doorway. Watching her. "I put them on this morning."

"Skip, this is silly. Really, I can take the couch. Just loan me a blanket."

He pushed off the doorjamb and entered the room, his big body snatching away her air in the process. "No, here you'll be closer to Michaela if she needs you in the night."

He had a point. The girls were sleeping together in Becky's queen at the end of the hall. Her daughter was beside herself with excitement. It would be a miracle if her eyes closed tonight.

"All right." Arms tight around her middle, Addie surveyed the L-shaped room with its panorama of windows, the sitting area with its fireplace, wine-colored love seat and rocker.

"Bathroom's in there." He nodded to a short hallway next to the closet. "Help yourself to the towels, shampoo—whatever you need."

The thought of standing under a spray, washing her hair, her *body,* in the same shower stall he'd stood in this morning...

"I need to check on Michaela," she said, walking quickly from the room. Down the hall, she quietly opened the door to Becky's room. Pegasus burned as a night-light in the corner opposite the bed, illuminating a path to where her child slept.

"Hi, Ms. M.," Becky whispered when Addie stood gazing down at the two bumps under the covers. One was tiny and curled into a ball; the other—closest to her—claimed a pre-puberty leanness and was almost Addie's size.

"Hey, Becky," Addie whispered in return, a smile on her lips. "Seems your roomie didn't last, huh?"

"She tried, but as soon as I started reading her a story, she zonked. I think the excitement of the storm, then sleeping over, wore her out."

"No doubt. Well, good night, then. If she causes any trouble in the night, don't hesitate to come for me."

"I will. 'Night."

Addie leaned across Becky and kissed Michaela's soft rosy cheek, then on an unexpected whim she touched her lips to the smooth forehead of Skip's child. "Sweet dreams," she whispered.

Slipping from the room, she gently closed the door.

Becky lay staring at the darkened wall across from her bed.

When had her mom last kissed her good-night?

She couldn't remember.

Was it the night before…before…her mom and Jesse had fought so hard and loud? The night her mom screamed for him to stop?

The night everything went wrong….

Oh, God, would she never forget the horror of those moments? The shouts and curses? Those moments she'd snuck from her room and stood in the hallway to the trailer's narrow kitchen?

Why, why, why had she crawled out of bed that night? Why hadn't she stayed where she was—like always—hiding under the covers, blocking the noise with her pillow?

Think of something nice. That's what her counselor advised when the images got bad.

Shivering, she reached a hand across the mattress and touched Michaela's arm, gently curling her fingers around the child's wrist. Michaela was real, warm and real.

Slowly, slowly, Becky's jitters faded.

Think nice things. Put yourself in a nice place.

Michaela was sweet and kind. She had a mother who loved her and worried about her, who kissed her good-night.

One day Ms. Malloy would see her grow up into an adult and be somebody. Like a nurse or a doctor or a ballerina.

Michaela could be Becky's lifeline of hope for a happy future.

On that thought, she closed her eyes and let pictures of Barbies and bees and Ms. Malloy's good-night fill her mind.

Back in Skip's bedroom—he was gone—Addie got ready for bed and pulled the drapes across the stormy night. After she removed the gym pants and sweatshirt Becky had loaned her, she folded the clothes and placed them on the cedar chest at the foot of the bed.

A pair of flannel teddy-bear pjs rested on the pillow. Had Skip set them there or had Becky?

What difference does it make? Just put them on.

The difference was if Skip had set them on the pillow, he knew what she'd have against her skin all night, in his bed.

Oh, for heaven's sake! Don't be so much of an idiot to think that you're on his mind. The man's probably dead to the world on his couch.

By the time she brushed her teeth with the new toothbrush she found in a clean glass on the sink's counter, crawled under the downy quilt and flicked the light, the alarm clock indicated 11:07 p.m.

The house was quiet, except for the rain drumming against the roof and windowpanes, and the wind whining around the rear porch. She tried not to think of whose bed she slept in, or that her head lay on his pillow.

She tried not to picture his big body, quite likely naked, in the very spot she occupied. She had seen him naked once.

The last time…

Home for Christmas after his first college semester, he'd wanted to see her the moment he unpacked his suitcase, and called her from his parents' house. The ferry lineups had been jam-packed with vehicles that Friday before the holiday and she had waited all afternoon in her room.

And then his voice came through the line. "Addie," he said. "I'm here. I can't wait to see you. Can we go somewhere?"

She heard the eagerness in his voice. He hadn't forgotten her, back here on Firewood Island finishing twelfth grade, while he was at the University of Washington.

Surrounded by college women.

In the end, there had been no place private that first week. But then came a day after the New Year when her sisters had returned to the mainland with friends, and Addie's parents had gone to Seattle to visit Charmaine's aging grandmother in a nursing home.

Sitting on her bicycle in a soft rain, Addie watched her parents drive onto the ferry, watched the ship sail away. Then, she raced back to the house. Within minutes, Skip entered the back door.

They kissed and touched and stripped from the kitchen right to her bedroom. And when they were both free of clothes, she stood in the center of her room, looking up at him with a shy smile. "Do you know this is the first time we've seen each other completely naked?"

"Mmm." He nuzzled her neck, nibbled at her lips. "You're so beautiful you hurt my eyes, Addie."

"Backatcha," she whispered, glorying in his admiration, his touch.

They'd made love all afternoon, using the three condoms he brought, but when time ran out, when the gloom of his departure in two days crowded into the room, they had clung to each other again—free and natural, relishing the true texture of their bodies.

In that fourth time, *that final time,* she'd conceived.

Eyes stinging, Addie turned onto her side in his enormous bed.

Her lost little baby, the one she'd carried under her heart so long ago, the one she'd worried about day and night, yearned for….

Oh, God. Never a day went by that she didn't think of that abandoned little daughter. *Where is she? Where is she? Where? Is? She?*

As always remorse and guilt and regret threatened to press her into a swirling abyss from which she could not climb free.

Gasping, she sat up. In the next instant, she tossed back the quilt and stumbled to the bathroom, where she heaved the sandwich Skip had made into the toilet.

She had barely rinsed her mouth when he appeared in the doorway, clad in a white T-shirt and a pair of loose gray sweats.

"Addie?" He was at her side immediately, arm around her waist. "What happened?"

"Nothing. Just…just a bad dream."

He peered into her face and she was glad the light was off. "You don't look well," he said.

So much for the darkness. "I'm fine."

Without releasing her waist, he helped her back to bed. There he tucked her in like a child before turning on the night lamp, and sitting next to her hip on the mattress.

"Addie." He kept her bandaged hand between his warm palms. "I'm going to help you with your house. Don't worry, okay?"

If the situation wasn't so bizarre, she might have laughed. He believed she'd worried herself into nausea about her house, when it was their child that had her stomach whirling like a wind eddy.

"It's not the…house." Her voice cracked.

Pressing her cold fingers to the soft, warm cloth on his thigh, he asked, "What then?"

"The baby."

"Baby?"

Shadows caught his cheek and mouth, and for a moment she saw Skip as he'd been that last afternoon standing in her bedroom with the rain whispering against the windows.

"Our baby," she said.

He went very still.

"Do you," she began, and in her ears her voice squeaked. "Do you ever think of our baby?"

"Addie."

"Do you, Skip?"

He looked away, sighed, turned back. His Adam's apple bobbed. "I'm so glad you asked," he said. *"So glad."* His gaze went to his thigh, where he turned her palm over and traced her heart line again and again. "There's something I need to tell you." He lifted his eyes and a chill skimmed her spine.

She came away from the pillow. "Do you know something? Do you know where she is? Is she all right?" Maybe with his connections, his money, he'd heard something, investigated—

"Addie...Oh, God, how to say this... Addie, she's here in—"

"Here?" She tore her hand away, grabbed his arm. "What do you mean *here*? Where? In Burnt Bend? *Where?*" She clambered to her knees. Her fingers clutched his T-shirt. *"Who—?"*

"It's Becky, Addie."

She didn't understand. Becky? What was he talking about? Becky was his wife's—or former partner's—daughter.

She shook her head. "No, I mean, *our* baby. The one I...we..."

His eyes didn't waver. Those honey-gold eyes she had loved when she was fifteen, sixteen, seventeen.

Until he'd deserted her. Until he'd said, *I can't do this.*

Slowly she released his shirt, her hands falling palms up in her lap. "Are you saying Becky isn't your wife's child?"

"I've never married."

Of course. Commitment wasn't his style. "But... How...?" Momentarily she stared at the door. Twenty feet down that hall slept two children.

And Skip was saying both were of her body, her womb. *Hers.*

It couldn't be. Couldn't. Fate could not be so sweet. So *cruel.*

She became conscious of her heart hounding her rib cage, pushing panic into her throat. She attempted a painful swallow as her gaze threaded back to him.

"I've wanted to tell you for over a year," he said. "But you were still married at the time. You had another child."

She couldn't believe this news, his rationale. Scrambling from the bed, she paced to the center of the room, pushing a hand through her hair.

"And you thought I wouldn't care? That I'd forgotten, given up?" Her lungs hurt, labored. As if she'd sprinted the Boston marathon. Uphill.

"No." He pushed off the bed. "But I'd heard stories about your husband."

"What stories?"

"That the marriage wasn't…strong. I didn't want to interfere or make things worse for you or your— For Michaela."

A caustic laugh burst from her throat. "Worse? How could it be worse? If Becky's my child—*my child*—"

God in heaven. The baby she'd mourned for half her life. The one she'd carried within her flesh. The little girl her arms had ached for, *still* ached for. Addie's gaze snapped to the bedroom door, to the obscure hallway. "Does she know who—?"

I am? The words hung in the shadows like specters.

"No," he said slowly. "I haven't told her."

Yet. Addie hugged her waist, shaking against the past that had haunted her nights, her days and every moment between. "What *does* she know?"

He drew his hands down his beard-stubbled cheeks. "That she was adopted from here. That I'm her biological dad. I'd heard something from my father a year and a half ago, just before he died. Something his lawyer mentioned. It prompted me to look for her." He sighed deeply. "I found her in foster care in Seattle. She'd been in the system for four years by then and was a ward of the state. The adopted father had relinquished her to the authorities and they were attempting to match her with another set of adopting parents."

Addie let out a small cry.

His fingers flexed, as though he wanted to reach for her. "Meantime," he went on, "Becky was in the process of trying to locate her real parents. Somehow, Dad got wind of it—I think through someone from the agency that took her when she was born. Anyway, he called me. I hired a lawyer, did the DNA tests and…" Driving his fingers into his hair, he held it off his forehead for several seconds. "As they say, the rest is history."

A cold wash of fear spread over Addie's skin. The dead mother.

"What happened to her…to the mother?"

Skip took a step. "Honey, let's talk about this in the morning. It's after midnight."

She backed away. "You drop this bomb in the middle of the night and then want to go to sleep? Uh-uh. Deal with it the way I have to. And don't treat me like some juvenile on your football team. I have a right to know. What happened to her parents?"

He walked to the door, closed it quietly. Leaning against the wood like a man beaten in battle, he said, "The father stabbed the mother in a fit of rage. They rushed her to the hospital, but she was dead on arrival. Jesse was charged and convicted and sentenced to life. He's been in the pen at Walla Walla for the past four years."

Jesse. The man her baby grew up calling dad.

Addie had a name at last, but it was useless now, useless because she could do nothing, couldn't breathe, couldn't hear for the thunder of her heart. "Becky?" she rasped.

Skip's eyes were tortured. "Addie, let's leave—"

"Damn you," she breathed. *"Becky?"*

"She…she witnessed the fight."

The fight. The murder.

In the silence that followed, Addie stared at the man across the room.

She tried to say something, anything. But her tongue wouldn't form the words, her throat couldn't produce the sound, and then his face went hazy and the last thing she remembered were his arms lifting her and his voice calling her name.

Chapter Seven

Skip carried Addie to the bed and pulled up the covers. He wasn't a doctor but he could see by those half-open blank eyes and slack mouth that she'd fainted. Wheeling around, he hurried to the washroom for a cool, damp washcloth. His hands shook. He had no idea if she was prone to fainting or if this was her first time. Whatever the case, he knew instinctively she'd be mortified at this kind of vulnerability around him.

Once more he sat at her hip. He wrapped a cool cloth around her right wrist, wiping a second one over her forehead and down her temples.

"Addie," he whispered, hoping to rouse her. Carefully, he pressed the washcloth against her pale cheeks. Concern spiking, he pulled back the covers, pushed a pillow under her knees. "Come on, honey, wake up."

At last her eyelids fluttered and he watched her pupils focus, first on something across the room, then slowly weave in his direction. For a fleeting instant, relief rushed through him.

She would be okay. Physically.

Emotionally… God only knew. She had endured thirteen years of heartache and guilt, and now this.

"Skip?"

He forced a smile. "I'm here, babe."

"I had the worst dream."

"You fainted." He took the cloths from her forehead and wrists. "Do you remember our conversation?"

Her eyes widened slightly and he saw she recalled it, recalled it all. "It's true? She's…?"

He dipped his chin.

Her eyes turned wintry with each beat of his heart. "When are you planning to tell her about me?" she asked.

"When it's right. When the two of you have had a chance to bond." He took a sustaining breath. "It's the reason I moved back to the island, Addie. Listen," he said when her face crumpled, and she covered it with both hands. "Let me make a cup of tea or something."

"*Nooo.*" Shaking her head, she turned onto her side, away from him, and coiled into a fetal position. "Leave me alone."

"Honey…"

Her arms came up, shielding her head. "Just go, Skip. I need to be alone."

He debated. His heart broke for her grief, for all the sorrow that would crowd her mind, her soul, through the night. She'd blame herself, because that was Addie. She'd been blaming herself for years. As he had. Hell, he still got nightmares over the horrors their little girl suffered.

But he'd also had ten months of joy with Becky, months in which he'd witnessed a massive change in his child's personality. Oh, she still went to counseling, but every day he observed the genuine happiness in her eyes. He saw her strength.

In this moment, Addie was where he'd been less than a year

ago, when he'd wanted to crawl in a deep, dark cave and never come out.

"All right," he said, rising to his feet. "If you need me for anything, I'll be in my office down the hall." The room he hadn't any real use for until now. Until Addie needed him in a way she never had before.

"I thought you were sleeping on the couch," she mumbled, but he caught the angry lilt to the words. She wanted him gone— far, far away.

"I've got a sleeping bag." No way was he going downstairs again. "See you in the morning," he said, and left the room on silent feet.

Besides, what did it matter where he laid his head tonight? His mind blazed with a hundred thousand scenarios of what tomorrow might bring. Front and foremost: how would Addie react to Becky?

Differently, a small voice nattered.

And that difference worried him as nothing had before.

Addie wanted to die.

She wanted to leap for joy.

Her tears held both. *Becky,* she thought as the sobs built, shaking her body with great hulking gulps.

Oooooh! The pain was enormous, slicing her soul from every angle.

Burrowing her face in the pillow, she curled tighter, 'til her knees touched her chest.

How could she not have known? How could she have missed her own child's uniqueness?

The bygone years pressed down, and she cried for the distress her baby had lived. With parents who had not given her precious child the home Addie's father promised thirteen years ago.

She cried for the moments she should have shared with her child: Becky's first smile, first tooth, first word. And all those treasured developing moments. *I should've been the one whose*

*hand she held that first day of kindergarten, of first grade. I
should have read the report cards, watched the soccer games or
piano recitals or swimming lessons that surely* they *would have
observed.*

But had they? In their raising, had those parents granted
Addie's cherished gift the chance to do the things she liked? To
choose avenues she enjoyed? Had they protected her against
wrong decisions?

Unlikely, her inner voice cried. From Skip's description,
sound parenting would've been a rare product in a home filled
with anger, where a mother was murdered.

Oh, Becky, Addie mourned on a fresh flow of tears. *I'm so
sorry-so-sorry-so-sorry.*

The guilt of her decision at eighteen threatened to crush her
as she listened to the storm rant outside. The wind howled in
sync with her soul, scattering a million thoughts through her
mind, but none as deviant as the acknowledgment that *she* could
have chosen differently. She could have fought harder against
her father's persistence.

A roller-coaster ride of "could haves"…with none reaching
a destination.

And so she lay, fatigued in body and spirit in Skip's bed,
waiting for the easement of the storm beyond the windows, for
flecks of dawn on the horizon and for her heart to quiet its insane
race.

Skip was up and showered before daylight. He hadn't slept.
Hadn't been able to close his eyes for ten seconds. She'd been
on his mind every minute; his ears tuned to the slightest of
sounds from across the hall. Twice he imagined her weeping, but
it was only the wind keening in the trees sheltering the house.

After yanking on a clean pair of jeans and a T-shirt, he tiptoed
down the staircase to the kitchen, where he started the coffee, a
dark roast blend of Seattle's Best. By the time he took his first

sip, a gray light announced the start of day. Though the storm had subsided, a drizzle glossed the flagstone steps and patted the earthen beds where he would grow nonflowering shrubs to thwart the interest of bees.

A soft thud had him looking over his shoulder. Arms around her waist, Addie stood in the doorway still wearing Becky's teddy-bear pajamas, and for an instant he mistook her for the child he'd reclaimed.

Until he saw her sleep-tumbled hair, the hair he'd yearned to thread his fingers into six hours ago…and the mouth he'd kissed as a teenager, the mouth he wanted to kiss now, as a man.

"Hey," he said. Last night their lives had shifted, and he was unsure where or how she would take that shift.

Her gaze sidled past him to take in the windows. "Storm's let up. I should get back to my place." But she remained in the doorway, motionless as a cornered mouse.

He walked to the cupboard. "Coffee's fresh," he said, and poured her a mug.

Still, she stood in the doorway.

He stirred in a teaspoon of creamer, the steadiness of his hands a contrast to his heart. He walked over to her with the steaming cup. "Addie…"

"No wonder she seemed a little vague about your reaction to bees when she went out to check the hives with us."

Skip shook his head. "This…family thing is still a learning process."

"And now there's me." Her arms stayed tight against her ribs; she didn't reach for the coffee, but instead shouldered a look toward the second floor. "I want to run upstairs, grab her and hold on forever." Her voice held a load of need, anxiety and hurt. "I want to pretend this never happened. No. To be weeks, months, a year down the road with all this behind me. I want…I want…" Eyes closed, she shook her head. "I want her to love me," she whispered.

Skip's heart rolled over. "She will, honey."

Her eyes latched on to his. "Do you think so?"

The stark eagerness in her voice tore him in half. It was an effort to smile. "What's not to love?"

She blinked as if coming awake and then she walked past him, past his round pine table, to the patio doors where daylight rose in ashen layers.

"I gave her up, Skip. *I* was the one, not you. I carried her for nine months and still...*still* signed the papers and let them cart her away like dirty laundry. I didn't look for her. I didn't rescue her. I did *nothing* for twelve years."

"Let me tell you a little secret," he said, coming up behind her. "Becky hated me the first two months we were together. Oh, she was glad to be out of foster care, but she had a chip the size of a football field on her shoulder. She didn't show it often— she'd gotten real good at hiding her emotions." His mouth twitched. "She's a lot like you that way. When the going gets tough—and I won't whitewash it, Addie—her tough *was* tough." He sighed. "When she felt threatened or hurt or angry, she'd lock herself in her room and not come out for two days. Any tiny thing could trigger it. The last time was when I told her to cap the toothpaste."

"Sometimes I see her watching me," he went on. "She still has issues she's working through with her counselor, but it's getting better. We created a strong girl, you and me."

He let that sink in.

She slowly turned. "Has she ever, you know, asked?"

About her real mother, about Addie.

He wouldn't lie to her. "Once. When I told her we were moving back to Burnt Bend. She knows I grew up here, so she asked if her birth mother came from the same town."

"What did you say?"

"That you did." He didn't add that Becky had gone into her "holing up" stage at that point. That it had taken him a day and a half to coax her out and when he did, he knew she would not ask again. But he also knew she had stored the information for another day, one well down the road, perhaps when she was mentally and emotionally ready. He wasn't sure their daughter was ready this time, but what was done was done. Addie knew and they needed to go forward with the decision he had made for them all.

"Why now, Skip?" Addie asked. "Why tell me at all? And why, for God's sake, in the middle of a storm after…after…"

After her house suffered considerable damage. Incapable of meeting the misery in her eyes, he stared at the floor. "Not telling you felt wrong." He lifted his head. "The guilt was driving me around the bend and I know that sounds selfish, but then…here you were under my roof." *Under my covers.* "I had to tell you."

"I can't say I grasp your logic. I'm too hurt. No matter that I was married, I had the right to know. *Then.*"

He bobbed his chin once. "I know. But my omission wasn't by malicious intent. I wasn't sure how your husband would react, or what he knew."

"He knew I'd given up a child." She scowled. "Who in this town didn't know? It was juicy gossip for years."

"I'm so sorry you had to go through that." *I should've been here for you,* he wanted to say. Though the words would only add salt to a wound that hadn't truly healed.

She rubbed her arms as if cold. "So what do you want to do?"

"It's not what I want, it's what you want, but since you asked I think it's best to give you both some time to get acquainted first."

She let out a long breath. "I agree." She moved past him. "I'll have that coffee now, then I need to wake Michaela and take care of my house."

"Why not let her sleep?" He glanced outside where dawn hovered, wet and glum. "It's barely light and miserable to boot."

"She'll be scared if I'm not here."

"Becky's with her," he countered.

"I can't expect Becky to do my job."

"It's not a job, Addie. Becky likes your daughter." He attempted a smile. "She's her sister. And, their friendship is mutual. Besides," he said, aiming for a little levity, "what kid wants to go out in the rain to a cold, damp house—which yours will be—when they can sit in their pjs, eat Cheerios and watch TV or play with their toys?"

She took several sips of coffee, evidently thinking over his rationale. When she checked the stove clock, he knew he'd won. "Fine. I'll leave Becky a note and pay for babysitting."

He ignored the latter. "I'll go with you."

"You've done enough."

For her house? Or about his disclosure concerning Becky? *I want to help,* he craved to say. *With everything.* But at this point she wouldn't want his help. She wouldn't want a damned thing from him.

He watched her dump the coffee remnants into the sink and rinse the mug. "It's my problem," she said. "I'll deal with it." On that note she walked out of the kitchen and up the stairs.

Looking at the empty doorway, Skip heard the shower come on in his private bath. If there was one thing he'd learned in the past two weeks, it was that Addie's years of struggle with Becky's adoption, a failed marriage and a stuttering child had granted her a formidable inner strength.

Skip rummaged in a drawer for a notebook to tell Becky he'd gone across the road. Addie wasn't the only one with a stubborn streak.

She heard the whine of the chain saw before she caught sight of his yellow slicker among the dark branches of the fallen hemlock.

The rain had lessened to a saunalike mist but without heat. On her approach, she noticed that a good portion of the tree had been cleared from the side of the house. The branch causing all the damage was gone, cut into four-foot lengths and tossed on a pile nearby.

Skip was bent over the main trunk, guiding the saw's blade through the next section. Blue smoke colored the air while sawdust streamed against his muscled, denim-clad legs and workman's boots.

The fact he had retired from the NFL hadn't deterred his will to keep in shape. She'd recognized the evidence last night when he'd picked her up as easily as a feather pillow and carried her to his bed. And then this morning in the kitchen, when he stood in that black crewneck T-shirt showcasing a chest that for years graced magazine and TV ads for cologne and polo shirts.

The trunk gave, twisted slightly and fell apart. Between Skip's broad, gloved hands the saw sputtered before he set a boot against the top section of the wood and zinged off another limb.

Becky's yellow slicker must have caught his attention; his head turned. Under the bill of a cap donning the logo of the Denver Broncos, the team he'd retired from, his eyes were as somber as the day. He killed the stuttering motor.

"Hey." That familiar crooked smile zapped electricity through her bones. "Thought I'd get a head start."

She walked closer. "I need some answers, Skip."

He set the chain saw on the grass. "Sure. Shoot."

"Tell me exactly how you found out about Becky from your dad."

He sighed. "It was something he said when I came home after he first got sick three years ago. Strange as it sounds, he'd never stopped thinking of his grandchild, wondering where she was, how she was doing."

Addie could relate a hundredfold.

Skip went on, "We were sitting at the kitchen table one night after he'd gone through another round of chemo, and he said Mom never got over our family's one big mistake."

Addie stood as motionless as stone. How could the senior Daltons have believed for one second Becky was a mistake?

Her thoughts must have shown in her expression, for he hurried on. "Dad thought a piece of Mom's heart died the day Becky was—" he swallowed "—adopted. And he'd been part of that. He'd been the one to contact the lawyer for your father."

Addie blinked. "What do you mean? I gave my baby to the adoption agency."

"A private agency, Addie."

"But that can't be." Her voice rose. "I signed the papers. I saw the papers. They were official. The woman from the state came and talked to me, explained the procedure."

"The woman worked for the lawyer. Oh, she was legit, he was legit. The agency was legit and had been doing business for thirty years. They just erred with *this* family. With Jesse Farmer."

Addie rubbed her forehead. Defeated, she looked at Skip. "How?"

"How does anything get screwed up? Someone miscalculated, misjudged, hadn't done their homework."

"Your father knew all this and didn't do anything?" She was horrified the man would keep his mouth shut for almost a decade.

Skip shook his head. "Our parents didn't know at the time, either. Dad was acquainted with the lawyer of the agency, that's all. Apparently, the guy had been someone from Bellingham, my mother's hometown. They'd grown up together."

"A regular reunion." Addie couldn't help the ice in her voice.

"My parents thought a private agency would be better. They figured kids fall through the cracks too often through state adoptions."

Addie studied her crumpled truck. "I never met the parents. I always wondered why I couldn't meet the parents. The agency lady, Darby Peters, said it was hard for them to travel because the mother suffered from agoraphobia, but that the woman was talking to a counselor and was making big strides in overcoming the problem." She shoved her hands into the slicker's pockets. "Darby told me that by the time the baby was born, the mother would be fine." She looked at the fallen tree, her broken house. "I was barely eighteen. What did I know?"

"It's not your fault. It's not anyone's fault, except the agency's."

"I should've been there for my baby."

"So should I. But we can't beat ourselves up over it." He came closer, and carried with him the scent of wood shavings and motor oil.

"What prompted you to look for her?" Addie wanted to know.

"About six months after Dad died I was injured on the field and had to retire. But I'd always wondered, too, where our baby had gone, and after talking to Dad, I hired a private investigator. He found Becky in a Tacoma foster home. She'd been shuffled around almost three years by then." He looked away and she saw the guilt in his down-turned mouth.

She wanted to reach out, console, *be consoled* in this terrible mesh of events.

He said, "When Jesse went to jail, Becky became state property…" He grimaced. "Thing is, people want babies, not half-grown children. Long story short, I went a little mad."

She could fill it all in. His millions. Securing connections in the ranks, rushing DNA testing.

For the first time she thanked his career for this small favor.

"I'm glad it was you," she said truthfully.

"Makes two of us."

The alternative would have put their child into another home with another family if Skip hadn't gone on that search.

He said, "I'd do anything for you and Becky to—"

She held up a hand. "Let's see how it goes, okay? For now, it's enough that she's two hundred yards away. Safe and loved."

His full-bloomed grin took her breath. "She is," he said. "I can't tell you how glad I am about that."

"I can see it in your face every time you look at her. You're a great father."

She watched him survey the house in the trees beyond the property.

He said, "I'm still feeling my way around that department."

"If it'll make you feel any better, we all are. There are no standards in parenting except love and kindness."

His head tilted slightly and creases fanned the corners of his eyes. "You've always been a smart lady, know that?"

"Smarts aren't all academia," she said, wanting this conversation over with. "I need to check inside, see if the power's come on." She walked around the corner of the house to the back door.

In the kitchen, she flicked the lights. Nothing—which meant trees still blocked the road. She checked the laundry room, shadowed in blue light from the tarp covering the ragged four-foot hole; the plastic screen had prevented the rain from causing more damage.

Thank you, Skip, she thought, listening to the wail of the chain saw. Much as she hated to admit, she and Michaela would have been in an awful state living alone on this road. The nearest neighbor was two miles to the east as the crow flew.

Inspecting the dryer—the branch had missed the washer by inches—she knew the machine was ready for the recycling truck. The wood had crushed the operating panel and dented the top of the barrel.

Addie had no idea where the money would come from to buy a new dryer. She had some savings and, because the house was old, a small amount of insurance on the dwelling, but first and foremost, she needed a new truck.

Biting back a swell of emotion, she headed for her bedroom and a change of clothes. Next on the agenda were her bees; to ensure the hives remained secure and the insects safe.

Before leaving the house, she tried the lights in the hallway and kitchen again. Still no power. Bundled in a warm sweater and fleece jacket under the slicker, she walked around to where Skip had cleared another section of the tree. Water dripped from his cap as he bent to drag several sawed branches to the pile.

"Skip, leave that. I'll hire a guy tomorrow." Zeb Jantz, a retired logger, would come if Addie asked; he'd do anything for Charmaine Wilson's daughters—just to get her to notice him.

Skip heaved the branches onto the heap. "It'll only take another half hour." He paused, his gaze probing hers. "You need to check the hives."

"Yes, but—"

He set the chain saw under the tarp. "Tell me what you need and we'll go in my pickup."

"A few frames and supers in case of damage. But you can't go."

He patted his belt where he kept the EpiPen secured. "Old faithful is just a shot away."

Too fatigued to argue, she nodded. The day was cold and wet; the bees would be sluggish, but if Skip stayed in his truck and parked at a distance of two hundred yards, there shouldn't be a problem. Still, she worried.

Fifteen minutes later, after Skip called Becky, they had the vehicle loaded and were driving the perimeter of the clover field three miles down the road. She could see the breakage the moment they crested a small knoll.

Two hives down, the supers and frames layered like cheese slices across the drenched grass. Addie's heart sank. The cost wasn't high, but on top of her home and truck, the wrecked hives had her hauling in a deep breath.

"Dammit," she whispered, grasping the door handle before Skip brought the truck to a stop.

"What can I do?" He stared through the windshield.

She took in his helpless expression. He could not leave the

confines of the vehicle. "Go home. When I'm done, I'll call you on my cell."

He turned his head, eyes flashing. "Understand this, Addie. I am not leaving you. Not today, not tomorrow. For better or worse, we're in this together." And then he was out the door, slamming it shut.

A shot of adrenaline spurred her to the rear of the vehicle after him. "Are you crazy?" she cried. "We're talking *bees* here, Skip."

Ignoring her outburst, he lifted the door. "It's raining. Cold weather chills their flight muscles and prohibits flying. I do my research."

"And have you forgotten their venom is a cocktail of melittin, apamine and a number of amino acid radicals?"

Dragging the stack of supers with empty honeycomb frames from the Toyota's bed, he said, "I'm not entirely stupid, Addie. I plan on living a few years yet, so caution is my middle name. Soon as we unload, I'll get back inside the truck."

She flung a look toward the hives. "I don't like it."

He stopped, his eyes as serious as the day he'd told her good-bye when he was twenty.

She sighed. "Fine. Hurry up then."

His mouth tweaked. "Giving me orders now?"

"Saving your life," she retorted, yanking on her white coveralls.

"You did that two weeks ago," he said softly. "When you said hi."

"I didn't say hi, you did. I asked what you wanted."

"Yeah." He tugged the next stack from the truck. "And all I could think was you. I wanted you. I have all my life."

All my life. Her heart lurched before her head snapped around. "Omigod, you never quit, do you?"

He frowned. "Quit what?"

"Lying through your teeth." She grabbed the smoker, then the supers from his hands. "'I wanted you all my life.' *Please.*

What *you* wanted was the NFL." She snorted. "But what ticks me off most is that for a second, for one damned second, I fell for it. *Argh!*"

Her bees, she needed her bees to calm her wild, angry pulse before she went screaming into the wet yonder. "Go home, Skip," she said. "I don't need you here."

Biting her tongue to avert the tears, she started around the truck.

Chapter Eight

"Dammit all, Addie." His hand whipped out, caught her arm and swung her around quick enough to spill the supers to the ground. She ignored them, captivated by the ferocity in his eyes, by the longing, desire and sorrow she saw there. Every emotion she'd buried when it came to him.

"I've never lied to you. Never. Even back then—whether or not you want to believe me. I wanted our baby. I wanted you. But my parents…"

"Yes, let's talk about your parents, Skip," she said, wrenching out of his hold as the first tear spilled. *Damn him.*

"There were circumstances…"

Circumstances. She almost laughed. The only circumstance was the Daltons had thought her unworthy of their son. Hadn't she overheard Ross Dalton tell his meat manager at Dalton Foods that Skip was destined for the big leagues? She'd stood a foot behind the man as he'd said, *Skip knows he needs to be free and clear of any unnecessary baggage.*

She'd been that unnecessary baggage.

A gasp or cry, she couldn't recall, had escaped her lips and Ross Dalton had turned. So she'd run, away from the grandfather of the baby she carried, away from the embarrassment, away from the Daltons. She hadn't stopped running until she married Dempsey.

His parents, he'd said. Oh, yes, his parents had ruled every decision concerning her, and they'd roped her parents into the fray.

Her throat hurt. Her heart hurt. She was barely conscious of Skip tugging her away from the fallen stack of supers, and stepping so close his slicker brushed the panels of her slicker. His fingers touched her cheek where tears of heartbreak fell and mingled with the rain.

"I'm so damned sorry," he said.

She shook her head. "You have no right to come back here and turn my world upside down again. No right."

"I couldn't stay away, Addie. Not after finding Becky and discovering you were single again. I just couldn't."

Naturally, he was right. She would have died knowing what she did about Becky. And if he hadn't included her, not put their child within easy access for her and Becky to unite, to bond…

Still, Addie ached to take a lengthy stride back and put some distance between them. Except his fingers had crept along her temple, into her hair, and his palm, his broad warm palm that had cupped so many footballs, secured her in place.

The distress in his eyes altered and yearning took over before desire flashed. Anchored by that one hand, she remained rooted to the spot, her heart a tolling bell in her chest.

And then he bent his head and set his lips against hers.

Cold and chaste as the kiss was, it communicated a thousand recollections of bygone kisses. The first, the last and all those in between: tender and impatient, erotic and romantic, and lastly, bittersweet.

And now there was this moment, this kiss in which she felt him hesitate for the first time, unsure of how she would respond.

She wanted to push him away.

She wanted to crawl into his skin.

In the end, her heart lunged through the tug-of-war in her mind and she lifted her hands to his shoulders, rose on her toes and kissed him back while the rain drummed against their heads, streamed down their cheeks and threaded along their lips.

He tasted of thirteen brokenhearted years and she couldn't get enough. Her fingers curved his neck. Her mind whirled. Somewhere deep inside her heart she called his name. And then…

He was setting her away. "Addie." His fingers shook on her cheek. "You were always a passionate woman. And so full of mystery."

If he'd doused her with a bucket of ice, her insanity couldn't have cleared quicker. "Passion is hearsay, Skip. Back then I was young, you were young. It was hormones, pure and simple. As for the mystery, here's an update." She bent to retrieve the supers she'd spilled. "I was never a mystery. I was Addie Wilson, an ordinary teenager who got hung up on a guy who didn't want her when the chips fell. Happens all the time. I went through it then, I see it at the high school today. You'll see it with the guys on your team. Except you'll be on their side, not the girls' side. Nothing new and certainly no ambiguity. Now, go wait in the truck."

Stack in hand, she tromped through the wet grass to the white boxes housing her extra income.

"Dammit, Addie." The frustration in his voice escalated because he couldn't follow her. "Don't you get it? I wasn't like those guys. I would've given it all up for us. I would've married you, but—"

"But you didn't. Now, be quiet. Docile or not, the bees will sense if I'm upset, and as much as I care for the little bugs, I don't like their stingers any more than you do."

"You kissed me back just now," he grumbled loud enough to carry across a couple hundred feet of rainy day. "That means something."

"All it means is I haven't been kissed in two years."

"You haven't?" She heard his surprise. Then he said, "Neither have I. Longer, in fact."

She let the comment pass. She needed to concentrate on her hives, not mull over the fact that he hadn't been with a woman for *that* long. The NFL's Skip Dalton had never been *without* a woman.

In her peripheral vision, she saw him pace in front of the truck, EpiPen in hand and heedless of the drizzle. "We're going to talk this out once we're done here," he stated.

"We'll see." Focusing on the two downed hives, she went to work, setting them right and retrieving the honey frames.

Please, she thought, noting dozens of dead bees squashed by the wet and damaged wood. *Let the queens be here.*

But her heart sank when she lifted the brood chamber and saw that both queens were gone—and that the colonies had vanished with them.

Where they'd flown was anyone's guess. Possibly when the hives tumbled, the wind had whipped the insects away, scattering their little bodies out across the field or into the trees. Or, if they'd been lucky, before the worst of the storm hit they had swarmed to seek shelter.

Because she'd known bees all her life, she prayed for the swarming, that at the moment her bees were somewhere safe, preparing to return. If not, the insects would die within days without their stored source of honey, or nutrition to keep the queens alive.

And if they didn't return… It wouldn't be the first time she lost a colony. Meantime, all she could do was restore the hives and collect the remaining honey from the apiary.

"Addie."

"I'm busy."

"I hate standing around doing nothing."

"Don't make me responsible for your life, Skip."

In the ensuing silence the drizzle pit-patted grass and ground. "For the record? You *were* a mystery. And I loved you for it. You weren't like the others. Never have been. I'd like us to have another chance. Is that so wrong?"

After thoroughly checking the honey-laden frames to guarantee there were no attached bees, she carried the damp frames to his truck, where he stood ready to take the batch from her arms. His hair lay plastered to his forehead; rain dripped from his strong nose, his bristly chin. The weather spiked his lashes. It was all she could do to keep from kissing him again.

"Skip." To distract herself, she spoke as though he were one of her less astute math students. "Last night's information overload is about all I can handle right now."

He handed over a new stack. "Have dinner with us tonight. My treat."

"No." She walked back to the damaged hives.

"Not sandwiches. A real dinner. Somewhere in Burnt Bend. There must be a place the girls would enjoy."

The girls. From now on her life and Skip's would revolve around the nuances of their children's friendship, their interaction with each other. More than anything Addie wanted Michaela to have a sister, to have Becky *be* that sister. One part of her heart leapt with joy, the other half shuddered at the thought of a potential negative reaction when Becky discovered she was in truth Michaela's sister.

What if the girl retracted her friendship?

The possibility sent a jolt of fear through Addie. Becky was her baby's first true friend, the only one who had been able to break through Michaela's stuttering. Addie could not deny the change toward a smoother dialogue each time the two were together.

She glanced to where Skip finally sat in the truck, though the window was open several inches. Her resolve caved.

"Dinner would be nice," she said. "But with the house and

my truck…these hives…" She swiped a hand over her face. "Another time, maybe."

"I've got more money than I know what to do with. I can have a crew at your place tomorrow."

Oh, God, he tempted her. But never again would she be dependent on a man. Dempsey hadn't liked her earning more than he did as a mechanic, had convinced her to quit teaching when Michaela was born. But when Dempsey walked out, Addie had walked on.

She'd gone to the school board, updated her resume and was rehired immediately. And she intended to continue teaching. Earning her own dollar, paying her own way, initiated a sense of pride she hadn't felt in years. She would not give that up again. She would make it through these last weeks of August if it took every penny of her meager nest of savings and insurance.

"I'm fine," she called, bending to care for her bees. And prayed she spoke the truth.

Through the windshield, Skip watched Addie work the hives with swift precision. The heavy rain and gusts of wind kept the insects in the undamaged hives from venturing outside, although the thought of one landing on him whipped apprehension down his spine.

To get his mind off the bees, he focused on Addie's lithe form in the slicker and tall rubber boots. The weather glued her ponytail to her back. Her slim bare hands pieced together the broken hives as if they were a child's building blocks.

At the first flash of lightning across the sky beyond the field, Skip counted the seconds—one and a half—before thunder boomed. Massive dark storm clouds rolled above the tree line, piling in with the rain. Again, he slid down the window. "Addie, we have to go."

"One minute."

"No. Now," he called as another streak limned the clouds and the rain pelted harder. "The girls are home alone. Becky hates lightning."

True or not, he didn't care. If it got Addie out of danger…

She strode toward his truck with the last load of honey frames and tossed the boxes into the back. Seconds later the tailgate slammed and she jumped into the passenger seat. Wipers battling the rain, he drove from the field and sped down the pavement toward home.

"I'm sorry." He glanced to where she sat swiping water from her face with cold, red hands. "It isn't fair, all this happening to you."

She'd lost so much while his property remained intact. And he could afford repairs.

She didn't respond, only looked out the window, and he had the feeling she contemplated his statement in another way, the one concerning the past.

They drove a half mile, the rain swishing against the tires, before she said, "I'm hoping my insurance will cover most of it."

Her voice held defeat. Skip reached for her hand, brought it to his thigh. He wanted to pull over, hold her and kiss her until they were both warm. Keeping his gaze on the road ahead, he said, "Before you say no, hear me out. You're right. I didn't fight hard enough against my dad and yours thirteen years ago. And at nineteen I should have known better. I was a man, not a boy. But I let my dad convince me. I let him run my life as always. He wanted an NFL star and…" He sighed. "I'll admit I wanted it, too." He looked over, saw he had her full attention.

His courage expanded. "But I wanted you more. I've always wanted you more. Trouble was, the macho jock you knew was also a coward. I listened to my dad." He gave a small humorless laugh. "Funny thing was, Mom never agreed. I'd hear her arguing with Dad in their bedroom to let me go."

"So why didn't you listen to *her?*" Addie asked quietly.

"Because I kept thinking what if he's right? What if I can't make a living for you and the baby? Truth is, I was scared out of my mind."

"And now you're not." A margin of sarcasm plucked at her voice, yet she left her hand in his.

"And now I'm not," he agreed.

She slipped her hand away; he felt the loss. She said, "So you'd like to atone, is that it?"

"In a nutshell. More though, I owe it to you and Becky to, I don't know, to set things right. The way I didn't back then." He slanted her a look. "Will you let me?"

They had reached their lanes and he pulled left, into hers. He drove straight to the honey shed, not slowing near her ruined truck and house. The mess had him swallowing hard; the bill would be in the thousands.

In front of the little building, he hauled out the honeycomb frames from the truck's bed while she unlocked the door and directed him inside to the tables, where he laid the stacks.

She had yet to respond to his question.

"So, will you?" he asked. "Let me help."

She was almost out the shed door, and when she turned her eyes were the color of the day's sky. "It doesn't work that way, Skip. You can't buy atonement."

Anger flickered behind his tongue. She *would* take it the wrong way.

"Is that what you think this is?"

"I don't know what to think anymore. So much has happened in the last twenty-four hours…."

Chancing it, he came toward her, touched her cheek. "It'll get better from here on," he said, watching her eyes close. He nearly kissed her again, but the last thing he wanted was for her to think all he had to offer was a sex-starved man. Although since their reunion—since seeing *her,* touching *her*—he'd come to believe in the phrase wholeheartedly.

Her eyes fluttered open. "I can't give you the answers you want."

"Not answers, just a little hope, is all." He tendered a smile.

"A little hope." She smiled in return. "For Becky I'm willing to try anything."

For Becky. He shouldn't feel the pinch of hurt. The reason he stood here in this honey house was for their daughter. For Becky he had returned to the island and sought out Addie. Their child took precedence in every aspect of his life. He should be glad Addie claimed the same priority.

So why did he suddenly feel abandoned?

Buck up, Skip. Imagine her suffering a hundred times worse when you moved away thirteen years ago.

Depressed, he followed her outside, into the rain.

She sent Skip back to his house to check on the children, while she began the process of extracting honey from the collected frames, plugging in the flat knife to heat and preparing the extractor.

Some time later, as she reached for the last honeycomb frame to slice off its wax caps with the knife, the door to the shed opened and Michaela bounded in with Becky on her heels.

"Mom," her daughter shouted. "Becky wants to see how we make honey. Mr. D-D-Dalton said she could. Isn't that neat?"

The girl in question—oh, God, her *other* baby, the one she had kissed last night for the first time in more than a decade—stood hesitantly at the door, a shy smile crossing her features. Features Addie suddenly saw were a mixture of her parents….

Addie's blue eyes, Skip's dark hair.

Her slightly flared ears and Skip's crooked left incisor.

That the child inherited Addie's wide mouth seemed a pity… until she zeroed in on its tilted-up corners. They were pure Skip.

"Is it okay, Ms. Malloy?" Becky asked, bringing Addie out of her reverie.

"Of course it is, love." The endearment slipped off her lips on a sweet swell of emotion.

Becky's smile bloomed. "Thank you."

The girl hurried across the floor to stand beside Michaela. They were two sisters, two children with Addie's blood in their veins. The thought had her heart on a joyous journey. Was this how Skip had felt when he saw their child for the first time in that foster home? When they'd had their first conversation?

Yes. From everything Addie had observed over the past week, Skip loved Becky—and was still in awe of her presence in his life.

"All right," she said, amazed by the composure in her voice. This was her moment to bond with her firstborn. One moment offered on a day when anguish appeared around every corner.

She said, "The primary job of the knife is to take off the wax. Otherwise you can't extract the honey." As she spoke she demonstrated before handing the knife to Becky. "Try it, but be careful. It's very hot."

Eagerly, the girl took the tool, working its edge as precisely as she had seen Addie do. "This is way cool," she said when the job was complete and the honeycomb stood ready for the extractor. "I never knew all this happens to the honey we buy in stores."

"It's done on a much larger scale with commercial beekeepers."

"A worker bee lives only two months," Michaela volunteered.

"Wow." Becky's eyes sparked. "That's *short.*"

Addie smiled. "And she only produces one-twelfth of a teaspoon of honey in her lifetime."

"You're kidding."

"That's why it takes eleven hundred bees to make a pint."

Becky stared as Addie set the last honeycomb inside the barrel of the extractor before securing the lid with its curved handle. "Michaela, show Becky where the clean jars are," she said, spinning the handle quickly.

"Okay, but watch, Becky!" The child ran for the shelf of one-pound jars. "The honey's gonna come outta the tap!"

"Cooool," Becky exclaimed as a thick, golden stream poured into the container. "Dad should see this."

"He has." Addie realized her mistake the instant Becky's eyes latched on to hers.

"Really? When?"

Intent on spinning the handle, Addie told Michaela, "Another jar, love." To Becky she said, "Years ago, when we were teenagers."

"When he was your boyfriend?"

Addie's fingers fumbled with the handle. "What makes you think he was my boyfriend?" Had Skip already told Becky about their relationship or was it a guess? Her heart climbed into her throat.

Becky said, "I asked him after we met you guys at the library."

"Oh? Why?"

"Because... Please don't take this wrong, Ms. Malloy, okay? But you and my dad don't...well, you don't seem to like each other."

Michaela wrinkled her pug nose. "Mommy d-d-d-does so like your d-d-d-dad, Becky."

"Not the way friends like each other." She cast a quick look in Addie's direction.

"That's not t-t-true!"

"Girls," Addie admonished. The last thing she wanted was for their friendship to disintegrate before it began. "Michaela, what Becky means is that Mr. Dalton and I knew each other a long, long time ago and back then—" How to explain? "We went to the same school but our—" *families* "—friends were different."

"You mean, they didn't hang out together?" Becky asked.

"In a way. It's a long story."

"I like long s-s-stories, Mom," Michaela offered.

Addie forced a smile. "Maybe another time, sweets."

Becky set another jar under the tap. "Did my dad do something bad to your friends?"

"He wasn't like that." Addie wished she could step around the extractor and hug this lovely, endearing child; reassure her that both she and Skip were different people today.

"Oh, whew!" Becky's shoulders drooped on a gusty sigh. "I thought maybe he was a bad guy and made fun of people and stuff."

"Not at all," Addie assured.

Except for the slogan that followed him around like a banner. *All girls are my girls.* How had she forgotten? She had watched him take the phrase into the NFL, dating women—spectacular women—at every turn.

I've wanted you all my life.

Oh, he'd been so solemn standing in her field of clover with the rain drenching his face, uttering words she'd longed to hear all *her* life.

Question was, could she believe him…this time?

Chapter Nine

The power was back by four o'clock that afternoon, and the road crews had removed the fallen trees blocking the access from her house to Burnt Bend. Addie was free to go into town and stay at Kat's.

She was inside Skip's kitchen when he set the keys to his truck in her palm and told her to use the vehicle until she could afford a new one.

"Kat has an old pickup," she stated. It sat in her sister's driveway where her husband parked it before he was killed three summers ago. Kat hadn't turned the motor in all that time, but Addie believed the truck would start with a little TLC.

She placed Skip's keys on the counter. "Thank you," she said. "For everything, but we'll be okay. Michaela," she called. The girls had disappeared into the recreational room the moment they returned from the honey house. "Time to go, button."

"Addie—" Tucking his hands under his arms, Skip leaned

against the counter. "Why not stay here? Michaela and Becky—"

She shook her head. "We've already taken up too much of your time, not to mention food and space and hospitality. I won't be anyone's liability." Like she'd been for Dempsey.

Skip frowned. "I like you being here. If I had my way," he went on, "I'd have you both live here." An edge of his mouth slanted upward.

"That isn't going to happen, Skip. Ever."

He sobered. "Am I so repugnant to you?"

She might have laughed—or cried—if the notion wasn't incredibly absurd. Looking at the maleness of him, at the richness of his hair, the hard high angle of his cheekbones, the shape of his lips and nose, the power in his shoulders…

Addie clamped the inside of her cheek to keep from blurting, *You're the most magnificent man I know! And I need to watch that I don't fall under your spell again.*

Instead, she gave him reality. "Becky comes first," she said, and saw he understood. What was between them took second spot in lieu of explaining Addie's relationship to their daughter.

When he didn't respond immediately, her breath slowed. Did he not want Becky to know, after all?

Thrusting the thought away, she pulled her cell phone from her jacket and said, "I need to call my sister."

"Where are you?" Kat asked when Addie requested her sister come get them.

"My place." She saw Skip's eyes narrow. Had he heard Kat's question?

"You're not at Skip Dalton's?" Kat asked. *Perceptive sister.*

Addie turned her back. "Yes and no. When can you get here?"

"Fifteen minutes."

"See you then." She snapped the phone shut.

"I could've taken you into town." Skip's voice was low—and was that a thread of disappointment?

She faced him. Not a muscle moved in his big body.

He said, "You're not a liability, Addie. You're—"

His words were cut off when Michaela, dressed in her pink jeans and a sunshine top that was Becky's, ran into the room. "Becky says I can stay with her tonight again, Mommy!"

"We're staying with Aunty Kat, button."

"Noooo," Michaela whined. "I wanna s-s-s-stay with Becky." The child wrapped her arms around Addie's waist. "P-p-please, M-M-Mom. *Pleeeease.*"

"Another time, Michaela." Gently, Addie set her daughter away. "Now, get your things. Aunty Kat is meeting us at the house."

"B-b-but I don't wanna go."

"Michaela."

"No." She stamped her foot. *"No!"*

Addie stared at her daughter. Never had Michaela acted out. From the moment Addie's marriage to Dempsey turned sour and he'd begun shouting and cursing and demanding, Michaela had withdrawn from the world around her, tucking away her emotions. That's when the stuttering began. And another part of her marriage disintegrated.

Can't she talk right? What's the matter with her? Dempsey's words.

"Michaela Jane," she said quietly now, aware they had an audience of two. "You will not speak in that tone of voice. Now, get your things. We are going home."

As quickly as it had advanced, the child's zest fizzled. "I'm s-s-s-sorry, M-M-M-Mommy. D-d-don't be m-m-m-mad."

Suddenly Skip hunkered down in front of Michaela. "Hey, pint," he said, summoning a big smile. "Mom's not mad. No one is. But tonight Mom needs you to visit your aunt because she's been real worried about you and Mom. The storm we had wrecked a lot of things, and she needs to know you're okay."

Michaela sniffed. "C-c-can't we t-t-t-tell her on the phone?"

"We could. But sometimes adults need to be in the same

room with the people they love. They need to see." He pointed at his eyes. "To talk." He touched his mouth. "To touch." Addie watched Skip brush a finger against Michaela's wrist. "Just to make sure everything is really okay."

"Like when I fall and cry and Mom asks a whole buncha questions?"

His smile was wonderful. "Yes," he conceded, and Addie knew it wasn't her daughter's comprehension that had delighted Skip as much as her flawless sentence. "That's it exactly."

"Okay." She took Addie's hand. "Let's go, Mommy. 'Bye, Becky. 'Bye, Mr. Dalton." She fluttered her fingers at Skip.

He hadn't moved off the floor. "How about you call me Skip? Mr. Dalton sounds sort of old."

"But you *are* old."

Behind Addie, Becky giggled.

"Well," Skip said slowly, as if taking the child's point to heart, "we can *pretend* I'm not old. And it'll be our secret, okay?"

"Mommy doesn't like secrets."

He glanced up at Addie. *Agreed,* his eyes told her, but to Michaela he said, "She's right. But in this case I think we're safe."

"Can I call him Skip, Mom?"

"Only if Becky calls me Addie." She smiled at her other child, her lost-and-now-found child.

Skip rocked on the balls of his feet. "Great idea. You okay with that, Bean?"

Their daughter shrugged. "Sure. But what about at school?"

Skip told both children, "In school, it's back to Mr. and Ms. How's that?"

The girls nodded. Knees popping, Skip stood. "Better get your stuff, pint," he said, running a hand over Michaela's hair. "Your Aunty Kat will be looking for you at Mom's house."

Worry flashed. "W-w-we shouldn't be late. C-come on,

Becky." The children dashed down the hall; their chattering faded.

For the strides he'd made with her little girl, Addie wanted to kiss Skip. "Do you realize," she said, unable to stop smiling, "how far she traveled a minute ago? You were incredible. As rotten as my luck has been in the last two days, today was a beautiful milestone. I won't forget it."

"Wasn't me. Michaela made the leap herself."

Addie stepped forward, set her hand on his cheek. "Maybe, but it was your gentleness that encouraged her."

For two heartbeats their eyes held. Then he asked, "What did he do to her, your ex?"

Addie let her hand drop. Mention of Dempsey sent a cold wash over her flesh. "He wasn't…patient with her."

"And you?" She sensed the ease of his voice belied a rising anger. "How was he with you?"

"I could deal with him."

"Did he hit you?"

"Oh, God, no. No, he wasn't like *that*. Things annoyed him at times, and Michaela internalized it as being her fault." It's what the school counselor pegged within the first session.

"What sort of things?" Skip's eyes held hers.

"What difference does it make? Dumb things. Little things." The way Addie made spinach salad with strawberries. Or the way she made the bed. Or how she stacked his beer in the fridge. A thousand trivial routines that irked him one day, but he'd ignore on another.

"Yet you stayed with him," Skip stated.

Something in his tone bothered her. "Don't judge me, Skip. There were a lot of variables involved you know nothing about."

He freed a long breath. "Sorry. I didn't mean for that to come out the way it did. You're right. I don't know where you've been in your marriage. But—" His features quieted. "I'm here, Addie. If you ever need to talk."

The children rushed back into the kitchen.

"Mom!" Michaela's brown eyes were animated. "Can Becky stay at Aunty Kat's, too?"

Addie's gaze whipped to Skip; his chin bobbed once. Her heart leapt. If she wanted Becky for a night, he would let her go.

The girl grabbed his hand. "Please, Dad, can I?"

"Why not?" The grin he tossed Addie held the sun.

"Yay!" Both kids cried in unison before charging back up the stairs to Becky's bedroom, yelling about what to pack.

"You okay?" Skip asked when they were alone again.

"No," she admitted. "I'm scared out of my mind. What if I do something wrong? Say something that makes her mad—"

The back of his hand caressed her cheek. "Just be yourself."

"Around her, I won't know how," she whispered, her heart clamoring, clamoring. What if she ruined their budding relationship?

"Yes, you will. Take it a minute at a time. Don't think any further ahead than that, and you'll be okay."

"It's different for a mother. *For me.* I carried her. I signed the papers. I watched them take her away."

"You were eighteen," he murmured. "Today's another day."

God in heaven, would she be able to deal with the questions from Kat and Lee—from Charmaine—when they saw Becky, saw the similarities?

This morning the girl had persisted with questions about the past. What if she cornered Addie's mother and asked the same questions? Could Charmaine be trusted to dodge the answers? *Can I trust myself not to spew out the whole messy story?*

She would have to; it needed to be told with Skip present.

"All right," she said, clasping her elbows. "Let's hope she's still talking to both of us tomorrow."

He leaned in, kissed her mouth, a quick touch of lips, not like the kiss in the field, but like a husband to his wife before he left for work. A kiss that was ordinary, yet singular because of its nature.

"It'll be fine, Addie," he said softly. "Have faith."

She would take his suggestion as a good omen.

An hour after Addie left with the girls, Skip drove through the misty rain to Burnt Bend and the grocery store his parents had managed for twenty-five years before his father died. Today, his mother was the manager.

He parked behind the building taking up the corner on First and Shore Road, a half block from the waters of Puget Sound, and thought how he hadn't visited the store since moving into the new house on Clover Road. In fact, rather than enter Dalton Foods the day he and Becky arrived to stay, he had brought several sacks of groceries from Seattle.

He hadn't wanted Becky to go through the wringer with his mother. Miriam Dalton had been too full of questions when Skip visited her three months ago, explaining his property purchase, his job change and that he planned to move back to the island with his daughter.

How did you find her? Does Addie know…? Miriam asked, astounded and hurt, he'd waited for things to settle before he told her about finding Becky. Questions Skip had answered as best he could to a mother with whom he hadn't spoken in almost a decade. Sitting in the kitchen of his childhood, he'd seen shame and guilt and remorse pool in his mother's eyes. The same feelings that had eaten at Skip for *his* part in the adoption.

That first meeting with Miriam broke years of ice between them, leaving Skip satisfied that their family could mend again. He'd hugged his mom with a promise to bring Becky around once they were settled, but not before his daughter and Addie had a chance to reconnect. Miriam hadn't argued, though her eyes had mourned. Becky was, after all, her only grandchild.

Climbing from the truck, Skip took a deep breath, then headed for the back door of the store, where he pressed the bell.

He wondered if the manager's office was still on the second level. As a boy he'd loved standing at the one-way glass window to watch the operation of the store.

A tall, skinny teenager opened the door. His eyes went wide. "Coach Dalton!"

Trying to place the boy, Skip smiled and held out a hand. "Sorry, have we met?"

"Nate Mosley." They shook. "Coach McLane introduced us at his retirement."

"Sure, now I remember." Skip stepped inside. "You're my quarterback."

"Yes, sir. Been with the team three years."

"You as good as they say?" Skip had gone over the players with McLane on numerous occasions.

The kid squared his shoulders. "Better."

Skip nodded. "Good start," he said, and saw the boy's ego fizzle a bit. "Maybe by the end of the season you'll be the best."

"I hope so, Coach. The NFL's all I think about."

Skip grunted. "Better think about your grades first, son, or you won't be on the team."

"Yes, sir."

"Mrs. Dalton around?"

"Up in her office."

Skip headed for the stairs. At the base, he turned. "By the way, Nate. Can you call the team, tell them first practice is next Wednesday at four?"

Nate's eyes lit. "Will do, Coach."

Skip took the stairs two at a time. The door to the office stood open a crack. Knocking lightly, he poked his head in.

Contrary to the clutter when his dad managed the store years ago, this office reeked of organization, every file and paper clip in its own spot. Miriam Dalton ran her job as she had their house during Skip's youth. For a minute, he watched the woman sitting behind an unfamiliar U-shaped desk. As always, her youthful appearance surprised him. She could pass for forty rather than mid-fifties. She had cut her hair in bob and wore a purple dress.

"Mom?"

She raised her head. "Skip!" Her gaze zoomed to the door, seeking Becky. "What a lovely surprise on a rainy afternoon."

He walked to the desk as she rose from the chair.

"I've been expecting you." Mild censure lay in her words though her arms wrapped his shoulders, and he kissed her cheek. "News whips around like the wind, especially when some of your boys work here."

"Met Nate a minute ago," he said, veering from her reproof.

"Yes, he reminds me of you at that age. Determined and focused."

"*The NFL's all I think about.*" Except Nate didn't knock up girls. Or hadn't yet.

Miriam pointed to one of three cushiony chairs circling a small coffee table. "Let's sit. Would you like a coffee or…?"

"Got a bottle of water?"

From a small fridge she pulled a bottle of Evian and handed it over before easing into one of the chairs. "I'm glad you're here, son."

She wanted to know about Becky, Skip could tell.

He sat, elbows to knees, the bottle dangling from his fingers, and came right to the point. "Becky's with Addie over at Kat's B and B for the night. Tree came down on Addie's house."

"Oh, no. Is there much damage?"

"Enough that she'll need a crew." *Aren't you going to ask if she's okay?*

"Will she be able to afford the repairs?"

Skip looked at his mother. Finances had always been the biggest object in the Dalton household. "If not, I'll loan her the money."

Miriam glanced away. "Yes, well. I suppose you can."

He was not going there. All the years he'd played pro ball,

Skip remembered his parents' mantra after a scout picked him from the college league. *"You're in the big leagues now. You'll be going places and seeing things far beyond this island."*

His father had slapped him on the back in this very office and said, *"You'll have your pick of women, son. Just be careful they're not gold diggers."*

One way or another they had all been gold diggers.

Except Addie.

She hadn't wanted a damn thing to do with him. Not when he'd phoned her after the adoption, just to see how she was faring because he'd been hollow with loneliness and so heartsick. And not when he tried to call again the following Christmas. No, what she'd said on that occasion was *If you ever contact me again, I'll slap a restraining order on you so fast your head will spin.*

It hadn't stopped him from thinking about her, from wanting to be with her, from loving her.

Miriam smiled. "You've done well, Skip. Can't deny I'm not proud. I just wish…"

"What, Mom? That I hadn't got Addie pregnant? That you're still worried someone might put two and two together, even though she went to the mainland, to that home for unwed mothers, finished her education and had Becky? Hell." He threw out his hands in an encompassing gesture. "Who here *doesn't* know about us?" The thought concerned him with school starting next week. Becky would meet kids whose parents remembered.

"Very few know," his mother said quietly. "Your father and I made sure of that."

Skip scowled. His dad—along with Addie's father—had done everything in his power to scoot her off the island…before the evidence was revealed.

Before Addie's belly grew.

"Yes," Miriam said. "We were worried that—that…"

"Say it, Mom. That it would affect business. People might point fingers and whisper, maybe stop buying from Dalton Foods. That's why you didn't want Addie here. Let's be honest."

"Yes, let's," she said, eyeing him. "This store was our livelihood. It put you through college, got you to the NFL." She studied her clasped, ringless hands in her lap. "I don't know how often I have to apologize, son. What we did… I know, it wasn't right." She looked away suddenly as a tear slid down her cheek. "I wish I could make it up to you."

Seeing his mother cry again shifted something inside Skip. He, too, had suffered over the estrangement he'd put between them. And then losing his father to cancer…

Skip set the water bottle, untouched, on the coffee table. "The past is what it is, Mom. You can't put something else in its place." He stood, prepared to leave. "I'll try to bring Becky around next week."

Miriam pushed slowly to her feet, and Skip realized how much his mother had aged.

"I'd like that," she said, wiping at the last of her tears.

"I might bring Addie and her little girl along with Becky. The girls have become pretty good friends."

Miriam's smile dimmed briefly. "That would be nice."

Skip studied his mother. All was well, as long as Addie and her family stayed *over there,* and he and his family remained *over here.*

Well, tough. Miriam would accept Addie as the mother of her grandchild, or the estrangement would continue into eternity. Skip would not give up Addie again. His mother had better understand that.

"Damn straight it's nice," he said, and strode for the door. Pausing on the threshold, he looked back. "I want us to be a family, Mom. I'm not asking your permission, I'm telling you. Maybe this time instead of a football, you can toss a little hope my way."

"Oh, son." Miriam covered her face, startling Skip. Concerned, he walked back to where she plopped onto the chair. Her eyes drenched, she said, "It's never been about football for me. Your father... He didn't want the same to happen to you as what happened to him."

"I don't follow."

She took a deep breath. "I'm forty-nine, Skip, not fifty-five."

Skip stared at his mother. Was she losing it?

"I was fifteen when I got pregnant, your father was twenty and, yes, we married, but Ross always felt stifled because of it, that he'd missed out on things." Miriam's mouth trembled. "He didn't want you carving the same path, and I wasn't strong enough to go against his wish."

Skip couldn't move. "Are you saying you had a loveless marriage?"

"No." She shook her head slowly. "But after you were born, we saw life differently. I'm not blaming him. I'm simply saying how it was." She sighed heavily. "In his senior year of college, he was a running back. The best. Major teams were talking to him, and then..."

And then they had a baby. But they had married and kept their child. A slow simmering rage fanned through his chest. "Except you did the opposite to what you asked of me."

Tears slipped down Miriam's face. "I couldn't give you up," she whispered.

As he and Addie had done with Becky.

He wanted to smash his fist onto the coffee table. He wanted to kick the chair. "How did *your* parents feel?"

"My father disowned me."

"But not dad's parents."

"No. They were glad because your grandfather always wanted Ross to take over the store. And when we had to marry..."

The son made his choice. His dad's store over the NFL.

Skip didn't know whether to hate his parents or himself more for his own weakness, his own cowardice.

"Son," Miriam said. She stood, went to wrap her arms around him. "Please forgive me for not being strong enough to stand in your corner."

All at once the logjam of anger broke away. Slowly, he set his arms around his mother, bowed his head to hers. "I can't fight this anymore." His heart felt battered.

"Then don't. Live for today, for now. For your little girl. And Addie." Miriam took his face between her hands. "Just be happy, son. Please."

He could do that.

The rain stopped by four-thirty and the sun broke through the clouds, warming the earth at once. Addie contacted Zeb Jantz to meet her at the house for a restoration estimate. Within minutes, she knew she could afford his price, and that he could repair the damage by the end of the week.

She breathed a sigh of relief. She did not want to be living with Kat when school began the following Tuesday.

Driving Kat's pickup back to town Addie thought of her sister's astonished look when she brought Becky to the B and B more than an hour ago and introduced the girl as Skip's daughter.

Kat had hidden her surprise, although Addie caught the intonation in her whispered, *"A daughter?"* once the children—including Kat's ten-year-old son, Blake—went off to watch cartoons.

Rather than responding, Addie had walked into the kitchen and called Zeb Jantz. Rushing out the door, she promised to explain everything when she returned.

Now, her heart pounded as she drove up the lane accessing her sister's timbered property. Before she could think it through, she brought the truck to a halt. Shielded by the trees, her sister's Victorian-style bed-and-breakfast waited. And so did Kat.

Come on, explaining Becky won't be that hard. Kat is not Lee.

No, thirteen years ago Lee had wanted to hunt down Skip and put a dagger between his ribs for bailing on Addie.

A nervous laugh escaped. She wouldn't put it past her older sister to pursue her original objective once she heard this latest news.

Addie let out a squeak as the passenger door suddenly opened and Kat jumped into the cab.

"Jeez," she cried. "You scared me silly."

"You'll live," her sister said mildly. "Now, 'fess up about Becky."

"There's nothing to 'fess. As I said, she's Skip's daughter."

"So why run a marathon to meet Zeb Jantz? And why are you sitting here hiding in the woods?"

Evading Kat's scrutiny, Addie looked down the road and gripped the steering wheel so tight her knuckles turned white. "I'm not hiding."

"Come on, sis," Kat said softly.

She couldn't breathe. An eternity passed. "She's my daughter."

Kat sat back in her seat. "I knew it."

Addie looked across the cab. "How?"

"Oh, honey. She has your eyes, your ears…the way she smiles."

"She smiles like Skip," Addie pointed out.

"Not always. And she has your tone of voice."

"Your imagination is running amok. Her voice is a young girl's, that's all."

"Maybe. Except I hear your inflections in it."

They sat in silence for several moments.

Addie whispered, "What if she doesn't like me when she finds out who I am?"

"What's not to like? You're a wonderful mother."

"Not to her."

"Don't shoulder all the blame. Others were involved. When are you planning to tell her?"

"Skip thinks it's best we get to know each other a little first." She looked over. "Can you keep this to yourself for a while?"

"It's not my place to tell."

"Thanks."

"And," Kat continued, "much as I hate to agree with anything Skip Dalton says, I think he's right. You and Becky need time."

Another pause ensued.

"He's not the same person, Kat."

"Of course he isn't. He's had years to fine-tune the charm and charisma with women."

Sighing, Addie gazed at the tree-shaded road. "I love you for being so protective, but you're wrong. He feels incredible guilt for what happened. He wanted to marry me, Kat. It was the pressure of his parents *and* my father that broke us up."

"Fine. I'll admit Cyril had a hand in the adoption decision—"

"More than a hand," Addie muttered, remembering her father's ranting about grades and futures and boys who couldn't keep their pants zipped....

You'll ruin your life, that's what you'll do, marrying that punk. In two years when the diapers pile up and the squalling never quits, he'll run like a bat outta hell. And then where will you be? You're smart, Addie. Top of your class. Make a smart decision. Don't throw away your career.

And then came the argument that tore most at her heart....

Think of your baby. Do you honestly believe you'll be able to give it the best home possible working a clerk's job or waiting tables in some hole-in-the-wall diner? Can you afford day care? Is that how you want your child raised, by some stranger, while you work two or three jobs to make ends meet? What kind of life is that for a child? Is that what you had, Addie? And what about Skip? You'll be taking away his chance at the NFL just the way you'll be taking your chance at becoming a doctor.

The "sensibility" theme tipped the scale in favor of signing the adoption papers. She'd had a secure and loving home. Yes, her dad had been querulous at times and her mother a meddler, but overall Addie had liked her childhood.

And then there was Skip. *Would* she be wrecking his prospects by agreeing to marry—as he first wanted? Would he eventually hate her for that choice? She never found out. While in her first trimester, he'd come to the house, glum and silent, and taken her for a ride in his beat-up Chevy, to the lake where they had first made love.

And he had done what she couldn't do.

He'd ended their relationship.

A week before her baby's birth, she signed the adoption papers—and let Becky go to unfit parents. *You didn't know!*

For that she would never forgive her father or herself.

In the passenger seat, Kat sighed. "Maybe it's best we put the past where it belongs. Rehashing it isn't going to change a darn thing."

She glanced at her sister. "Oh, Kat. You're still wondering, aren't you?" About who your father was and why Charmaine has guarded that bit of information so carefully all these years. The secret had put bitterness in Kat's heart toward their mother in the same way Lee despised *her* father for walking away from his family when she was three years old. The way Dempsey had done to Addie and Michaela.

Of the three men, Cyril Wilson, Addie's father and the last of Charmaine's husbands, was the only one who'd stuck around 'til the end.

"I haven't wondered any more than you did with Becky before Skip brought her home," Kat said.

Home. The word set Addie's heart aflutter. Becky *was* home. At last. At long last.

"You're right." She put the truck in gear. "And no matter how many years went by, it was never okay."

Never okay that she'd had to worry—helplessly—about the possible misfortunes her baby could endure. Misfortunes, like dysfunctional families.

Oh, Addie. As if your own family marched down the glory road.

But they weren't murderers.

None she knew about, anyway.

Kat set a hand on Addie's arm. "One day, sis. One day we'll be there. I know we will."

Be there. When all the questions were answered and all the heartaches healed. She drove to where their children skipped rope on the sunny porch of Kat's Country Cabin.

Chapter Ten

The dream sucked at Becky, pulling her deeper and deeper into the horror she watched from afar.

Her mom…screaming, fighting, battling. Arms flailing, legs kicking. Her father…standing over her in the kitchen. Shouting cruel words. His face twisted in drunken rage.

Becky couldn't understand his meaning. She only knew she had to flee, had to run out of the house, out of their lives.

Her mouth opened to get air, to yell for help. *Mommy!*

Blackness surrounded her. She couldn't see, couldn't hear a sound. Where was she? On the street? In a field? In the woods?

She stumbled forward, waving her arms at the murkiness so she didn't smack into a tree or a building.

Someone was calling her. Someone with a kind voice.

Mommy…?

No, her mother was gone.

Please, don't go. Don't let him get me.

She jerked awake, panting, her heart beating hard and fast as if she'd sprinted around the school track ten times. The blackness ebbed and in its place entered the softness of night—and her bed.

"Becky."

She blinked, her eyes focusing, finding outlines through the dark: the door, dresser, the window with its lacy curtains.

On the nightstand the digital clock read 1:04 a.m.

"You okay, honey?" the voice in her dream murmured.

Remembering, she turned her head. She was staying at the bed-and-breakfast place, the Country Cabin—and sharing a bedroom with Michaela.

By the light of the moon at the window, Becky recognized Addie leaning over the bed. She wore a pair of pale pajamas. "You were dreaming," she said softly. "Was it bad?"

"Yeah." Becky wanted the memories to vanish forever, but they always returned and they always sat like fat ugly toads in the back of her mind, sometimes for days.

"If you need to talk…"

"It's okay," she said, blinking away the straggling bits, wanting to talk to Addie. She seemed like a nice lady. And she loved Michaela. That was really important to Becky. She didn't like parents who were mean to their kids, or to each other the way Jesse had been to her mom.

"Slip over for a sec," Addie said, and when Becky moved to the middle of the bed without disturbing Michaela, the woman lay on the bed's edge, on top of the quilt. A moment later her fingers curved around Becky's. Tears stung her eyes. Addie was doing what her mom would've done to make the nightmare go away.

Except Addie wasn't her mom.

The thought brought more tears, until she had to swipe her wrist under her runny nose.

For a long minute they lay motionless. Addie didn't take her hand away. And she didn't talk.

Slowly, Becky relaxed; the tears dried. In a croaky voice, she said, "I was dreaming about my mom."

Addie waited, saying nothing. Becky liked that she didn't jump in with a bunch of questions. She relaxed even more. "My dad—Jesse—killed my mom. He stabbed her with a steak knife. I—I can't eat steak now." She sniffed. "I didn't see it, but I was there before he—he... Before I ran away. To the neighbor's trailer." Addie's fingers tightened, just a hint, and Becky's throat felt less full.

"Jesse... He'd—he'd grabbed the knife from the wooden block. Mom used to love baking bread," Becky rambled on, trying to think of her mom laughing. "She'd make a bunch of loaves and freeze them. Really good bread, y'know? With lots of whole grains and stuff. On the days she baked the whole house smelled like a bakery.

"Jesse loved the smell and so did I. Then she'd take a loaf from the oven and slice the end piece off and load it with butter and give it to me. I loved the end crust. Lots of people don't, but I did. It was crunchy and soft at the same time. It's the best part of the bread."

Becky let the seconds tick by, but still, Addie said nothing. "Her name was Hedy. It means delightful and sweet. I looked it up last year when Kirsten—she's my best friend—was into finding name meanings. Hedy... It's sort of old-fashioned, but it suited Mom. She had this really sweet smile, y'know? And she was always happy."

"Hedy is a pretty name, honey, and it makes me very glad your mom was such a nice person," Addie said, and she sounded sad.

Becky didn't want to think sad things anymore. "Do you bake bread?" she asked.

"I do. Michaela loves it with butter and honey."

Becky imagined the taste. Honey fresh from Addie's bees.

"If you want, I'll bake you a loaf or two and you can take them home with a couple jars of honey."

"Sounds yummy. Do you think Dad likes honey even though he's allergic to bees?"

"He loves honey."

Becky wondered how Addie knew so much about her dad. Probably because they had grown up on the island and went to the same schools.

Maybe one day she'd have a friend she could share stuff with from childhood. Somebody, but not Kirsten. Kirsten would never live on the island, never share birthdays. Becky would be thirteen on September twenty-first. Not so old that she couldn't have a friend for life if she and her dad lived on Firewood Island forever.

She was friends with Michaela. Okay, Addie's daughter was five years younger, but when they were in their twenties, it wouldn't seem so different. At least she didn't think so. Her mom's best friend—Aunt Clair to Becky—was almost nine years older than Mom.

She said, "I like Blake. Michaela's lucky to have him for a cousin."

Another long minute passed. "I should have stopped Jesse from hurting Mom," she said, and her voice sounded like when she was five. "I should've—should've…hit him or something to…to get him to stop. But all I did was run away."

"Oh, baby. Don't you *ever* believe that," Addie said, her voice stern, but loving. "You are not at fault for what Jesse did, okay?"

"That's what my counselor keeps saying."

"And she's one hundred percent right. She knows what she's talking about. If you trust no one else on this, trust her, all right?"

"That's what Dad says, too."

"He wouldn't steer you wrong, Becky."

She began to feel better—and sleepy. "Thanks, Ms. M.—Addie."

"You're welcome."

Becky yawned widely. "Can we bake bread soon?"

"The minute my house gets fixed."

"Okay." Her eyes slid closed. "'Night, Addie."

"'Night, honey."

Becky smiled. *Honey.* Her mom nicknamed her honeypot back when *Winnie the Pooh* was Becky's favorite bedtime story. And, like Addie, she used to hold her hand when Becky was afraid of the boogeyman. Addie sure seemed an awful lot like her own mom.

Thank goodness Skip wasn't anything like Jesse.

When her child's breathing deepened, Addie slipped from the bed and walked to the window. The rain had stopped, leaving behind a cuticle moon topping the timber on the hill behind the B and B.

While she couldn't clearly see the back garden, Addie recognized Kat's green thumb. Every flower common to the island flourished in the beds encompassing the bricked patio and patch of grass between house and hill. Roses, delphiniums, asters, hydrangeas, brown-eyed Susans, phlox, coral-bells…the list went on and on.

A haven to be sure, where the work-weary and retired could rest and enjoy a fragment of island serenity. Tonight, however, the thought of that serenity evaded Addie.

Down the hallway from Kat's living room where Addie slept on the couch, she had awakened, sensing something was wrong, and had come straight to the girls' room. At first she thought it was Michaela calling for her, but it was Becky thrashing through a dream.

About her mother's murder. *Hedy.* A happy woman who had been the mainstay for Becky in a house of misery.

Tears pricked Addie's eyes. She was so thankful—*so thankful*—Becky hadn't actually witnessed Hedy's violent death but, instead, the child had run outside to pound on a neighbor's door.

But, oh, God, she'd sensed Jesse's intent.

The thought shook Addie. Becky had been eight, a year older than Michaela.

Fingers trembling, she mopped at her tears and turned from

the window. After softly kissing both girls on the cheek, she left the bedroom to walk silently to the kitchen, where she flicked on the range light. Cordless in hand, she sat on a stool at Kat's spacious butcher-block island. Unconcerned of the time on the wall clock—1:32 a.m.—she dialed Skip's number.

"Bean?" His voice was gritty with sleep.

"It's Addie."

She heard the beat of confusion, pictured him snapping awake, propelling himself onto an elbow. "Is Becky…?"

"She had a nightmare."

"Ah, hell."

Addie heard him grunt as if he'd swung back the covers and climbed out of bed. "She's back asleep," she told him. "Oh, Skip. She told me about… About her mother's— God, it's making me ill to my stomach to think our little girl went through that."

"I hear you," he said, his voice as rough as bark.

She pinched her eyes closed, stemmed another flow of tears. "We… We talked a little. I didn't ask questions. I think she just needed to talk."

"You're good for her, Addie. She never talks after a nightmare."

Her heart gave a little hop. Not with happiness—who could be happy about a child's trauma?—but because Skip had given her hope that this time she might have done something right for her firstborn. That *this time* she hadn't failed Becky.

"It shook me," she admitted. "It always will. I could barely speak when she'd ask me a question. And afterward… After she'd gone to sleep… Skip, I wanted to beg her forgiveness. I wanted to…to walk over hot coals if it meant taking away her pain and those dreadful memories. I wanted…" Again her eyes filled and she reached for the tissue box on the counter. "I hate myself so much for giving her up and letting this happen."

"Addie, listen." His voice held a force she hadn't heard before. "We can curse ourselves about the past until we're sick.

But that won't help Becky. It isn't going to bring back Hedy, or erase the memories of that night. You need to be strong. And be there when she needs you. That's all either of us can do."

"She wants me to bake bread for her."

"She does, huh?" His smile filtered through the line.

"I'm going to teach her how. I want to give her something she can do with her hands whenever the hurt gets too much."

He was quiet, then said, "Only a mother would think of that. You won't fail, Addie."

"Baking bread is nothing compared to being there every day and for every mistake or hurt or confusion."

"Think I'll be there for every one? She'll be a teenager in a month. That alone will have her suffering things I'll never know or understand."

Addie sighed. "True."

"Give yourself some credit. You were there tonight. You've been in her life a little more than two weeks and already she's turning to you in ways she has yet to do with me after ten months."

"I'm not trying to take her away from you, Skip."

"Good." Anger punched into his voice. "Because if that's why you think I'm here, to dangle her in front of you like some fish on a hook, you are so far out in left field— Dammit, Addie." She heard his heels drum the hardwood in his room. "Don't you get it? I *want* you in her life. If I had my way, we'd…" An explosive sigh.

"We'd what?"

"Get married. Like we should've done years ago."

Her breath halted. Was he proposing? She rubbed her forehead. And why now, for God's sake? They didn't know each other, not anymore. Their lives were different. Yes, he'd be coaching the high school team, and teaching chemistry seventy feet down the hall from her, but their lives lay poles apart.

"Addie, did you hear me?"

"Yes." She swallowed back her fear. "It wouldn't work, Skip. We're practically strangers."

"We've known each other since grade school."

"What about the last thirteen years?" Why was she going on about this? She was not, *not* marrying him—nor anyone else, for that matter.

"What about those years?" he asked. "They're history. But we aren't." Again the sigh. "I've never stopped thinking about you."

She shook her head, chuffed a laugh, remembered the women, the beautiful, stunning women. "Oh, don't even go there."

He was silent long enough for her to think he'd hung up. Then quietly he said, "They weren't you, Addie. They were never you."

Words. Letters of the alphabet strung together for her comprehension. Except these words, *his* words, she did not comprehend. She said, "We don't love each other anymore. If we ever did."

"I loved you."

The certainty in which he spoke streamed through her, an invisible power that lodged a knot in her chest.

"But not today," she replied. "Good night, Skip."

"Are you so sure?"

Again he'd taken her breath. "It's too late for this conversation."

"Are you sure?" he repeated.

In all honesty she wasn't sure of anything. Not him, or the oncoming day, or what the future held with her broken house, or the girl down the hall. "It's two o'clock. I need to get some sleep."

"Marry me, Addie."

Oh, the hurt. He could not be this callous. "Stop right there. We have two children to think about. I will not upset Michaela— or Becky—by marrying someone I don't love." *Liar, Addie! You've loved him since you were thirteen.* Becky's age soon.

"Right," he said. "What was I thinking? Good night, Addie." He hung up.

Damn. She gazed at the phone. She hadn't wanted the conversation to end with bruised feelings. She hit redial.

"I need to go to Seattle tomorrow," she said without preamble when he answered, "to buy another truck. Would you like to come along? Kat or my mother could watch the kids for the day." When he didn't respond immediately, the constriction in her chest moved to her throat. "I'd like us to be friends again, Skip. Maybe we could start there?"

"All right," he said slowly. "When would you like to go?"

The tension in her stomach dissolved. "After breakfast. After we explain the trip to the girls."

"I'll be there at eight. And Addie? You've always had me as a friend." This time the phone hummed gently in her ear.

She sat listening to the night before finally rising from the stool to flick off the stove light.

Warm under the duvet on the couch, she heard the rain begin again, pattering on the roof, the sound comforting…the way his last words comforted her heart.

At seven the next morning Addie explained her plans about buying a new truck to Kat while they sat in the family kitchen eating cereal and fruit.

"Skip's coming with me," she said, and ignored Kat's raised brows. "I'm going to ask Mom to look after the girls."

"Let them stay here," Kat said. This morning she'd pulled her mahogany hair into a stubby ponytail. "I'm taking Blake to the pool this afternoon. He'll love the company."

"Sure?"

"Positive. I have only one guest and he's leaving before lunch. So take your time over there. If you need tomorrow, too, do it. Don't buy the first thing you see."

Staying overnight in Seattle with Skip? The idea had Addie flushing, quivering. "I don't think—"

"That's the trouble, sis. You think too much. Spending an

evening with Skip—hell, a night—might be just what you guys need."

"Kat, for God's sake. Yesterday you were all for me kicking Skip in the butt, now you want me to stay the night with him?"

Over the brim of her coffee mug, her sister's brown eyes bored into Addie's. "I've changed my mind. There's a child between you. Maybe it's time you had some frank discussions about that. Without interruptions." She set down her mug. "And maybe you need to see what's left between you."

"We're opting for friendship for now."

"For now." Kat ate a strawberry. "Talk to me tomorrow, after you've had a night alone with him."

"Kat," Addie admonished. "I'm not going to Seattle to sleep with him."

"Who said anything about sleeping? But—" her eyes were animated "—consider this. A lot of major issues have been resolved with a bit of pillow talk."

Addie stared at her sister. "What's got into you?"

"No, honey. It's what's gotten into *you*. You've been on a cliff since he came back. And now this thing with Becky… You're crazy about her."

"Does it show that much?" Addie murmured.

"Oh, yeah. Your eyes follow her every move. And if she says anything, you hang on her words."

"It kills me to think how much I've missed."

"Don't you think Skip feels the same?" Kat said quietly. "Don't you think he's got guilt issues? Have you ever asked him why he went looking for her?"

"Not really," Addie whispered. Not the deep-down reason. "I've been…" *Too wrapped in my own heartache.* "I just want her in my life," she said simply.

Kat reached across the table, laid her hand over Addie's. "I know you do. That's why you need to take the night. Sort it all out so you each know where you stand and what you want for her. Now, go pluck your eyebrows, do something cute with your hair and get ready. He'll be here before you know it."

Upon Skip's arrival, Michaela barely kissed Addie goodbye.

"Whoa," she said, feeling a twinge of abandonment. Gently, she turned her daughter around. "Not so fast, young lady. You do exactly as Aunty Kat says, okay? No silly stuff."

"Okay, Mom."

Touching Michaela's hair, Addie glanced at Becky. No vestiges of the dream, of the heartrending discussion last night, lingered in the older girl's eyes. Instead, she shot a grin over her shoulder, called, "Later, Dad," and disappeared up the stairs to the playroom with the other two children.

How could Addie not chuckle over their glee? Kat had promised a swim at the pool, an afternoon of cookie baking, a library trip and a pizza fest at suppertime.

Skip's mouth quirked. "Never thought I'd feel like second fiddle."

Kat laughed. "Get used to it. By the way, it's nice to see you again, Skip."

"Same goes."

Addie watched them shake hands. God, he smelled good. Like the woods and fields she loved.

His gaze returned to her. "Ready?"

Momentarily reluctant to leave, she scanned the empty kitchen. Since Michaela's birth, Addie had never left her daughter for more than a few hours and she'd always been within five minutes traveling distance. Today would be a landmark. For them both.

"Go." Kat ushered Addie and Skip out the door, shoved their jackets into their hands. "I need to cook breakfast for my guests. Call me later." With a wink, she shut the door.

Addie stood beside Skip on the stoop. The storm had vanished. This morning offered cerulean skies and balmy temperatures. But none of it held her attention. She'd done as Kat suggested. She'd fixed her eyebrows and hair and put on one of her sister's summer skirts.

For me, she told herself. *Not for him.* Except her heart said different when she saw how he looked at her—as if he wanted to nibble on every visible part of her skin.

"You cut your hair," she said, bringing the focus back to him.

No longer touching the collar of the blue polo shirt he donned today, his earth-toned hair lay in a style she immediately admired, longish on top, short at the sides and back.

"Yesterday," he replied. "When I came into town to meet with Cheryl Mosley to discuss the annual goals for the science department."

"How'd it go?" She would not think about him working with a former girlfriend.

He shrugged. "I'm sure she'd rather I teach elsewhere, but that's not going to happen."

"No?"

"No," he said firmly, then his grin turned impish. "So, does the hair pass?"

Without thinking, she reached up and pushed her fingers into the crown, where sunshine glimmered. For a heartbeat their eyes held.

"Addie."

"I…" Words failed. *I've always loved your hair… I love how you smell… You make my heart beat funny…* She saw he wanted to kiss her as much as she wanted to kiss him.

Gruffly he said, "We need to catch the ferry," and set a hand to the small of her back to guide her to his car. "Might as well ride in comfort," he said, opening the passenger door of the Prius.

They drove to the ferry landing in silence. There he pulled up, fourteenth in line to board, and remained close-mouthed. Her peripheral vision caught the shift of his muscular thighs as he stretched his legs.

Today he wore a pair of fashionably faded jeans and leather loafers. His feet were bare; dark hair dusted the arches. Years ago, she had seen him completely naked. With the sight of his bare feet resurrecting those moments, an arrow of heat stabbed her belly.

To dispense her diffidence, she said, "You haven't said a word for ten minutes."

He took in the car in front of them. "I want to kiss you, Addie. More than I remember ever wanting to kiss a woman."

"Oh." More heat. She touched her tongue to her lip, ran a finger along the strap of the purse in her lap. "So do I. You, I mean."

"I know." He said it artlessly, without ego or smugness.

He turned his head and his dark gaze skimmed her body, from the crown of her hair—which she'd let wave down her back— to her yellow tank top and tan skirt, down her bare legs to her yellow Camper Twins shoes. "You look incredible," he said. "More beautiful than I remember."

Her skin warmed. "Thanks. I don't often have a chance to dress up." Now why had she said that? He'd think she had no life.

And that was a surprise? Except for teaching, when was the last time she'd dressed for a man?

Heck, when was the last time a man looked at her with any curiosity? Dempsey, nine years ago—for about ten minutes, if she were honest with herself.

"That being the case—" Skip's presence pushed Dempsey into the distance. "I'll take you to dinner every week so you have an excuse to wear your pretty clothes."

Vehicles began to move onto the ferry. "Not necessary," she said.

"I'd like to, anyway." He drove into the parking hull, found a spot and shut off the motor. Reaching behind, he took their jackets from the rear seat. "Want to stand on the upper deck, have the wind blow in our faces?"

Oh, yes, Addie wanted very much to do exactly that. To stand there with Skip sounded fun and adventurous.

When the ship was underway, they climbed the stairs to the top deck and went out a side door. The sun was brilliant, the wind warm and the water flecked with diamonds. Farther out, two seagulls floated among the foot-high waves, while closer a small flock flew leisurely beside the ship.

Addie gripped the railing and laughed. "This is wonderful. Do you always come out here when you ride the ferry?"

"Depends on the weather."

"I could get addicted."

From behind, he set his arms around her waist. "Me, too," he murmured, and she knew he wasn't talking ferry rides.

Suddenly, she admitted what she had suppressed for years.

She loved Skip Dalton.

And it had nothing to do with the scent of the sea, nothing to do with the contented gulls, the sparkling waves or the way the wind whipped his dark brown hair back from his forehead. It was her skin shivering at the sound of his voice, her pulse racing at the sight of him, her breath rushing at his touch.

She leaned against his chest, felt his embrace—and for the first time since she was seventeen, bliss stole her heart.

Chapter Eleven

By noon they still hadn't found a truck she liked or could afford and Skip could sense her frustration building.

"Let's have lunch and consider the options," he said when they drove away from the fourth dealership.

"What options?"

"Food first."

She rested her head against the seat. "Fine."

To get her mind off her worries, he selected the functional chaos of Pike Place Market.

"I could spend a week here and never see enough," she said, her blue eyes finally full of the delight he'd hoped to achieve.

"It's one of my favorite spots in Seattle." Taking her hand, he led her down the cobblestone street to the Main Arcade.

There they watched the fishmongers tossing salmon at the Pike Place Fish Company, and decided that next time they would bring Becky and Michaela to see Rachel the Bronze Piggy Bank and the street performers along Post Alley.

He took her to the Sisters Café where they ate focaccia sandwiches and bowls of homemade clam chowder. Skip watched the pleasure cross Addie's face, yet her first thought was always of the children.

"They would love this," she'd say, or "I can just imagine their eyes...."

Oh, he could imagine, too. All he had to do was look at Addie.

Meal finished, they toured the day booths. Addie bought the girls trinkets and told him that someday—when she acquired the money—she hoped to rent a booth and sell her honey at Pike Place.

He laid his arm across her shoulders, tucked her close. She smelled great, a blend of sunshine and ocean wind. "If you want to do it this fall, I can loan you the money."

"Thanks, Skip. Don't take this wrong, but I won't be obliged to you or anyone. I pay my own way."

"Understood, except there goes my option proposal." Smiling, he ignored the tension slipping across her shoulders.

"Which was?" Wariness narrowed her eyes.

Feigning an ease he didn't feel, he continued to wander the noisy street. "That if you can't find a good used truck, I'll buy you a new one, which," he added hurriedly, "you'd pay back through affordable increments without interest."

She stopped, turned so his arm fell away. Pushing a hand through her hair, she sighed. "Look. I really appreciate your offer, but I will not now or ever be dependent on a man again."

"Is that what your ex did? Keep you dependent?" The questions were trapped between them before he considered the consequences—that she would tell him to mind his own business.

Instead, she looked away. "He tried."

Behind them, a man strummed a guitar and sang the blues. The dark lyrics fit Skip's mood. Every day, he discovered another facet about the kind of life Addie had endured while he played football, basked in fan idolization and lived at the high end of style.

If he could obliterate it all, including the bank accounts, to have had her and Becky at his side throughout the past decade, he would.

"Tell me about him, Addie."

She began walking again. "He was ten years older and managed Burnt Bend Auto Repairs as one of their main mechanics."

"How did you meet him?"

"I needed a new water pump for my car. He installed it and when I came to pay, he asked if I'd like to go for a coffee. We chatted and he seemed more knowledgeable about world issues than I expected."

"Him being blue collar and all."

"Yes, snooty as it sounds. And he looked a lot like someone I remembered." She shot him a look.

Skip almost stumbled. "You married him because he looked like me?"

"Sometimes desperation will make you do things you don't recognize are wrong."

Guilt bit hard. He thought of his mother's disclosure concerning her marriage to his father, about their skewed view of the future, of *his* future.

"And," she continued, "I liked his smile. It reached his eyes. Plus, he had a wit, which I needed."

Yes, Skip imagined she would've needed laughter in her life during those days. "Were you teaching then?"

"Tenth-grade science and math. Which sometimes intimidated Dempsey. He was clever in world politics, but he had difficulty with numbers. He'd barely completed high school."

Skip understood Dempsey Malloy's sense of inadequacy. Sometimes, he'd felt helpless beside the girl who had jumped a grade in elementary school and took advanced math in high school.

Addie should have had her future in medicine, a future she'd wanted since she was five years old and able to do seventh-grade math.

She said, "When Michaela was born he wanted me to be a stay-at-home mother. I agreed."

And no doubt fell into a routine that got harder to break with the passing years. "He didn't want you to go back to work," Skip observed.

"No. He thought it was great that I took over the bees when my dad died. It was a job he could understand."

And it put you on equal par, Skip thought. He wished Dempsey Malloy had never laid eyes on Addie. "What attracted him to you?"

"My mouth."

He snorted a laugh. "Your mouth?"

"He thought I was a good kisser."

Jealousy bashed like a fist. Of course, she had kissed the man. On hundreds more occasions than she'd kissed Skip.

He would not contemplate *where* Malloy had kissed Addie.

Skip guided her across Western Avenue toward the parking lot; time to continue the truck hunt. "Did you love him?" he asked casually, though his breathing labored.

"Not at first. But eventually I realized there were different levels of love." She cast him a look. "What about you? Did you fall in love with someone?"

"No. There were women, nice women, but…" How could he describe it? How could he say *I compared all of them to you?* She wouldn't believe him, not with his reputation still fresh in her mind, a reputation he'd created by flaunting those women, as well as his status. "It didn't happen."

He opened the passenger door of his car. "Maybe," she said, "it was meant to be. Had you been involved or married, you might never have bothered looking for Becky."

"You're probably right," he admitted.

She smiled, laid her hand against his cheek. "I think we've both suffered enough, don't you?" With that, she got into the car.

He walked around, slid behind the wheel. Staring ahead, he said, "I'll never hurt you again, Addie."

"Oh, Skip. That's an impossible promise. We'll hurt each other again, there's no getting around it, if…" Her eyes gripped his.

"If what?" he asked softly.

Pink spread across her cheeks. "We begin again."

Having a relationship. The words swayed between them. His lips bowed. Leaning over the console, he slid his fingers under her hair at the back of her neck, kissed her, feather touches here, then there.

And when she opened her mouth he moved in, let his tongue speak the language rushing into his groin.

Her taste spiced his blood, dizzied his head. He curved her hair behind her ear, pulled the lobe gently into his mouth.

"Addie," he whispered. When her small hand settled on his thigh, he thought he would explode. On a groan, he caught her fingers and brought them to his mouth. "I want to make love with you again," he said against her fingertips, and kissed each separately, lost in her. *I love you,* he wanted to say, but worried she would retreat, physically. Emotionally.

"We were…" Her throat moved. "We were going to check two more dealerships."

"Yeah." He sighed. There was the matter of her truck.

"Skip." Her fingers squeezed his hand. "When the time's right, it'll happen."

To make love.

For him the right time was now. All they needed was a room, a bed and privacy. But he'd promised to find her a vehicle.

"I know." He kissed her again. A soft, sweet touch of lips.

After turning the ignition, he backed out of the stall and drove from the Pike Place Market.

At a stoplight, she said quietly, "Maybe tonight." She smiled shyly.

"Okay." His throat closed.

Focusing on the traffic, he heard his heart thump in his ears. Fact was had she asked him to wait a lifetime, he would've agreed.

But he much preferred *maybe tonight.*

At five-thirty, Addie found a small green crew cab truck in excellent condition with low mileage and a price she could afford.

"You'll never find a better truck," the salesman—Derrick, according to his gold name tag—told her.

She didn't like him. Thirty minutes he'd been hovering at her shoulder, pressuring her with his litany of "wonderful pluses" as she checked out the vehicles that caught her interest.

To cut their search time in half, Skip had gone across the street to the Dodge dealership, while she explored the Fords.

"You're not familiar with trucks, are you?" Derrick asked.

"I've owned one before," she said.

"Did you buy it?"

"I got it from my father."

He smirked. "Most ladies get vehicles from the men in their families."

Pompous ass. If he called her the little woman, she was out of there—after she told him what he could do with his trucks.

But she wanted this vehicle. "What's your best offer?"

"Oh, we can't go lower than what's listed. That's a rock-bottom price you won't beat anywhere."

"Five thousand less?" she insisted.

Derrick shook his head. "Ma'am, you obviously don't know prices. A jewel of a truck like this—"

"Problems?" Skip asked, coming to stand beside Addie.

The man stared. "Hey, aren't you Skip Dalton from the Broncos?"

"Long time ago."

Derrick stuck out his hand, as well as his chest. "Welcome, Mr. Dalton. We get a lot of celebrities looking for vehicles."

"You like this truck?" Skip asked Addie.

"It might work."

Derrick said to Skip, "I was just telling the little lady that she'd be getting a real prize. Give me an offer and we'll see if we have a match."

Skip didn't hesitate. "Six thou off."

The salesman's smile cooled. "I'll see what we can do, Mr. Dalton. Would you like to take it for a test drive?"

"We would. And, Derrick? Don't call my friend 'the little lady' if—" he smiled lazily "—you don't want her calling you the little man."

Addie bit her lip to hold back her laughter as the salesman scurried off. "That was worth the price," she said.

His eyes flashed anger. "I hate arrogance, especially when it involves guys in the company of women."

Her humor died. "I was handling him, Skip."

"You shouldn't have to *handle* anyone. And for damn sure not jerks like him."

A splinter of ire poked. Did he think her life would be trouble-free now that he'd entered the picture? "Are you planning to run to my rescue every time?"

"That's not the point."

"Isn't it? You rescued Becky, and now you want to rescue me every chance you get." Vexed, she started for the dealership offices.

"Is that so wrong?" he called after her.

She turned. "I won't be your means to an apology and I won't make you mine."

"Jeez, I hope not. I think we've done our share of apologizing." He walked toward her, touched her cheek with the back of one large knuckle. "You matter to me, Addie. That's what this is about. You don't have to like what I say or do. Question is, can you accept it?"

"For Becky, I'll do anything."

He frowned. "I don't want you accepting me for Becky's sake. She's as much yours as mine. I have no ownership over her. If you would rather have nothing to do with me, just say so. It won't change what you hope to develop with Becky. I'd never interfere in that."

In his eyes there was truth, and it humbled her. "I'm sorry."

"Don't be." His smile was sad. The lowering sun washed shadows onto his jaw, darkening the day's beard growth that had lightly scratched her skin during their kiss at Pike Place, and suddenly she was tempted to step forward and set her mouth on his, but he was nodding to the auto-dealer offices. "Our guy is coming with a license plate."

Forty minutes later, the paperwork done and the extras such as new floor mats and mud flaps included, she drove her new pickup from the lot and followed Skip's Prius to an Italian restaurant along the waterfront for dinner. There she called Kat.

"We're catching the eight-thirty ferry," she told her sister. "We'll be there to pick up the girls around nine-thirty. I want to check out the house first, see how much Zeb got done today."

"It's all done, except for the inside work and replacing the dryer," Kat informed her.

"Really?" Addie had thought it would take the retired logger several days to repair the outside wall alone.

"Well, I haven't seen it, but that's what he said when he came by an hour ago. Look, why not stay there? The kids are settled watching *Eight Below* with a load of popcorn."

"I can't do that to you, Kat. You have a business to run."

"I have one new customer and she's leaving on Sunday. Besides the girls asked and I said yes."

Addie looked across the table at Skip, who was pouring the beer they'd ordered into a pair of glasses. "You don't play fair."

"Take this night, Addie. Do it."

She turned sideways, pretending to look at the lights on the water, and lowered her voice. "What do I tell the kids?"

"No problem. I've already told them you'll be sleeping in your own house to make sure the repairs to the wall are safe. Michaela worried the wind might blow it in."

"You put her up to that, didn't you?"

Kat giggled. "I take the fifth."

Addie glanced at Skip watching her with those melted-honey eyes. "Let me talk to the girls."

"Have a great night, sis," Kat said. "It's time." Then she called to the children and both Addie and Skip barely got a word in amidst their excitement to be staying another night with Kat and Blake.

When Addie closed her cell phone, Skip chuckled. "Hate to admit it, but they didn't sound too homesick for us."

"Not one bit." On one hand, Addie was pleased for her little girl; prior years had not been easy. Tonight, however, Michaela enunciated with clarity. She was conquering her hurdles. Yet Addie couldn't halt her stomach from wringing, or her mind from repeating Kat's word—*it's time*—like a news scroll line.

Skip sipped his beer, set the glass down again. "Tonight will go only where you want it to, Addie."

"I know that."

"You're nervous."

She glanced up. "How so?"

"You keep tapping the side of your glass."

She stopped. "And you're not nervous?"

"About spending the night with you, no. That you'll decide against it? Very much."

And she saw the veracity in his words when he lifted his beer with an indiscernible tremble. "Then we're even," she said, tucking a wing of hair behind her ear. When he laughed, she liked its soft bass sound.

"You've got the control, Addie," he said. "Use it."

"Or lose it?"

Reaching to take her hands, he looked into her eyes for a long beat. "Never. Be the woman you want."

That was when she recognized that he'd never been like Dempsey. For starters, Skip had darker hair and a softer mouth. The manner in which he carried himself was poles apart from Dempsey. The way he spoke. The kindness in his eyes…

She had married the illusion of Skip when she had said *I do* to Dempsey Malloy.

Most significantly, Skip would never ask her to give up teaching, or treat his daughter with disdain.

She'd been so very foolish.

"Let's order," she said. "Then go home to your house."

His eyes answered the smile in her heart. "Let's do that."

Night had fallen by the time she pulled her new truck into her front yard. Before she settled in for the night—*before Skip*—she wanted to check the repairs.

The beam of the flashlight indicated the tree had been stacked into a neat pile of logs, the gaping root hole filled. Jantz had cleared away the ruins of the wall, patched the aperture made by the tree. The exterior of the house looked as it had before the storm. The handyman knew his work. If not for her crumpled van, Addie could almost believe the storm had detoured her property.

Inside, the laundry room remained as Kat described, though Jantz had moved the wrecked dryer into the hallway.

"Couple days and it'll be as good as new," Skip observed behind her in the doorway. When he laid a hand on her shoulder, she stepped forward, nerves sensitized to his proximity, the scent of him eddying in her lungs.

"Let's move the washer so Zeb can get at that window wall first thing in the morning." She reached across the lid to the console and tugged.

"Whoa." Skip stepped behind her, gently pushing her aside. "You'll pull the panel right off doing that."

He wrapped his arms around the machine, muscles bunching and stretching under the short sleeves of the polo shirt, and inched the washer forward until it sat several feet free from the wall.

Addie reached in to shut off the water spigot at the wall and Skip bent to disconnect the draining hose. Their bodies bumped. Turning her head to say she was sorry, she saw that he leaned above her, his face within kissing distance. Seconds was all it took. Seconds for her to notice how the harsh lighting magnified the beard shadow on his jaw and upper lip, the arc of his lashes, the tiny rise at the summit of his nose.

His gaze came around and for two heartbeats he held her rapt.

She could hear her breath; feel his. A hot wash streaked up her thighs and she recognized the same intensity tighten the skin across his cheeks.

She wanted him. She wanted him *now*.

"Addie," he murmured, understanding.

One word. Her name. The spell snapped.

She jumped to her feet. "Thanks for the help, Skip."

He frowned. "You're welcome."

She hurried from the laundry. "I think it's best you go home."

He followed her into the kitchen, stood across the room. "Something wrong?"

He deserved an explanation—after all, she'd agreed, hadn't she? Back in Seattle she'd let him think they would spend the night together. But now that the moment had come…

"I can't," she said, fear biting her heels. Fear that, in the end, he would walk away again. That he wouldn't care enough, wouldn't love her enough. *Wouldn't have changed enough.* "Please understand."

The room yawned wider and wider, until a canyon lay between them.

He said slowly, "You want me to go." Then walked to the back door, where he paused to pull out his wallet and extract a tiny square of paper. Setting it on the counter, he held her immobile with his eyes. "Thirteen years, but I didn't forget. Not a single day."

The back door closed softly behind him.

Long, silent minutes passed before she summoned the courage. Curved in the shape of the wallet riding his hip, the page had been folded a half-dozen times.

Fingers trembling, she picked up the bulky pink two-inch square. Without reading the contents, she knew it was a note.

A note containing creases and frayed edges and dried dots where the tears had dripped. Her tears.

She remembered the day, the hour, the moment her pen had moved across the page, spilling her words, her heart.

Because…that day she had given up his child.

Because as much as she hated him, she loved him more.

So, she had written the note. And he'd kept it.

Through blurry eyes, she carefully unfolded the page. A tiny picture lay in its center, a photo he'd taken of her on a sunny day down by the lake where they made love for the first time. She'd worn shorts, a tank top and sat on a patch of grass, arms wrapped around her knees, eyes squinting against the light. She'd been laughing.

In those days, they had laughed a lot.

Nudging the photograph aside, she began to read, the words transporting her back, back…

Sept. 21, 1995

Dear Skip,

Today at 5:38 a.m. you became the father of a little girl. She was born after a long night of labor. I never stopped thinking that you should have been there through all the crying and cursing. But especially when she was born. She has thick, black hair and I can see the shape of your mouth. I counted all her fingers and toes.

The nurses laid her in my arms for a few minutes before they took her away. I can't describe the pain of that moment. It will be with me until I die.

My dad says the adopting couple has wanted a baby for eleven years. I think they'll give her a good home and love her very much.

Anyway, I thought you should know.
Take care,
Addie
PS—You don't need to reply.

With a shaky breath, she refolded the letter around the picture, the one he had chosen to carry with him every day, and knew what she had to do.

Chapter Twelve

Skip was toweling his hair after his shower when the phone rang. Noting the time on his bedside clock, he strode naked across the room.

"Addie," he said, reading call display.

"Can you come over?" There was a small quiver in her voice.

Had she read the note? Cried? It hadn't been his mission to make her cry; he'd simply wanted her to know he remembered, that she'd been in his heart. Always. "I'll be there in five minutes."

After setting the receiver back, he tossed the towel on the floor, went to the laundry room and dug a pair of jeans and a green sweatshirt with more wrinkles than a dried apple from the dryer. Minutes later, dressed, his damp hair finger-combed, he strode out the front door, flashlight beaming the way down the lane.

A cool night breeze brought the pungent approach of autumn and the faint scent of surf. Above the serrated silhouette of trees, the moon hung like an engraved silver plate.

He shivered at the sight. God, he'd missed Firewood Island. The moon, the billion winking stars, the smell of the woods and ocean… They were all Addie. She loved this tiny piece of the planet in a way that had humbled him as a kid, and still did when he recalled her standing on the ferry deck this morning, filled with happiness as the wind whisked her cheeks and hair.

Simplicity. That had been his Addie. *His Addie.* He nearly stumbled. Dammit, she was his, and he was going to prove it to her if it took all night.

There could be only one reason she wanted him to return to her house and that was to discuss Becky. But not tonight. Tonight he was talking about *them.* About him and her. About the possibility of marriage. He wanted to marry her, wanted it since he was eighteen years old, almost half his life.

He leaped onto her front stoop and reached to ring the bell. She must have been watching for him because the door swung open before he touched the lit dial.

She was dressed in a silky ankle-length robe the color of fine whiskey—like her hair. His first impulse was to touch the loose waves where they lay over her shoulders and trailed to her breasts.

He shoved his fingers into his pockets. "Hey." His smile failed.

Without a word, she swung the door wider, an invitation, and he stepped inside before she closed it again. For several tense breaths, they stared at each other.

"You read the note." His voice cracked.

She nodded, her gaze riveted on his, and he fell into the blueness of her eyes.

A foot, maybe less, separated them. If he leaned down, his mouth would fit hers, his chest would brush her breasts. And still, he did nothing, just let himself drown in those eyes.

He saw her swallow, clamp her bottom lip. She said, "I love you, Skip. I've never stopped."

Between his ribs, his heart flailed. His body shook. Years he had waited, years he'd believed she wanted nothing to do with him.

Reaching, he pulled her into his arms, tenderly kissed her mouth, her eyes, where tears swelled. "Let me show you how much you've been in my heart. How much I've missed you. Please, Addie."

She took his hand and led him down the hallway, to her bedroom where, in the glow of the night lamp, he caught a hint of yellow walls and frilly curtains, a four-poster bed with fluffy green pillows and comforter, before she turned, took his face in her hands and kissed him as if he'd just returned from ten years of combat. And maybe he had.

It was all he could do not to throw her on the bed, ravage her until the stars winked out. He wanted hard and fast, and he wanted it now. With other women he'd done just that, done what they'd requested, done the nasty—as they'd called it.

But this was Addie, the woman of his child, of his soul. The woman he loved beyond comprehension.

His fingers shook as he touched her hair, face, lips. Slowly, he unbelted the robe, pushed it from her shoulders to drop on the hardwood floor. She wore nothing underneath and he was in awe.

"Addie." His throat hurt. She was beautiful, like a piece of fine jewelry or china.

"I'm not the same, Skip." She remained motionless as she spoke. "Having babies changes a woman, makes her thicker in spots."

Taking her hands, he held them out, away from her body. "Ah, sweetheart. Those are the best spots. The best."

He let his gaze wander from the apex of her thighs to the softness of her belly, and up to breasts fuller than they had been at seventeen. And there it was, the little mole he remembered, on the curve of the left one. Leaning in, he set his mouth there and heard her sigh.

"I want to see you," she told him when his hands cupped her hips and pulled her closer, when he delved into her secrets. *"Skip."*

"In a minute."

She laughed softly. "No fair."

"You're right, it isn't." He swung her up into his arms and laid her on the bed. "I've changed, too, sweetheart. Got a few scars now." Mainly from the surgeries to his wrecked shoulder that wrecked his career. *For the better, Skip, because now you have Addie and Becky and Michaela.*

He yanked the shirt over his head, dragged down his jeans, kicked them aside.

Her eyes went wide. "You aren't wearing…"

"Underwear. I know. When you called I'd just showered. I grabbed what I could."

Amusement lit her eyes. "Which you found in the dryer."

His knee dipped the bed. "How'd you guess? Now, where were we?"

She set a palm against his chest. "In the night table there's protection. From my marriage," she added. "They haven't expired."

"Oh, hell." Closing his eyes, he hung his head. "I'm sorry. I was in such a rush to come over, I forgot… Addie, I never forget. Never."

Her eyes darkened. He could imagine what she was thinking. Since that Christmas when she conceived he hadn't forgotten to wear condoms. "Oh, honey. That came out wrong."

"No," she said. "We can't keep worrying about what we say for fear it might reflect on the past. Open the drawer, Skip."

He breathed again. "Soon." Then he covered her body with his and kissed her for a long time, his tongue moving in sync with his hips.

"I wish," he said, lifting his head, "that we'd never done it the first time in my truck. I should've taken better care of you, found a nicer place."

"I'm glad we did it beside the lake," she countered. "It was beautiful and special and unique."

"Do you know I fell in love with you at first sight?" Again he kissed her mouth, danced with her tongue, sucked gently on her chin.

"When we were in grade school?" She hadn't known that.

"It was the year they put the fifth, sixth and seventh graders all in one room because enrollment was down. You were in fifth and did seventh-grade math with us. I remember thinking, 'Wow, isn't Addie Wilson something? Not only is she pretty and smart, but she's really, really nice.'"

"You're making that up."

"It's the truth. Then one day when I was in tenth grade I saw you in the bleachers watching a game, and I fumbled the ball. I knew then you were it. You'd always been it."

She stroked the curve of his spine, the taut flesh of his butt. "Want to know a secret? When the bee stung you on the playground the year we were in class together and they had to rush you to the medical clinic, I thought you were the bravest boy I'd ever known. I haven't stopped dreaming about you since."

"Ah, Addie… So many years lost."

"But no more."

"No more," he agreed, and kissed her collarbone. He kissed his way up and down her body, graphing the changes as he went, his blood thickening in his veins, tightening every cell and nerve. He slowed his pace, then sped it up. Entwining their legs, he moved with her across the quilt, caged her hands above her head, kissed her breasts. He sat her in his lap, stroked his fingers into her secret spot until she moaned and he groaned and sweat beaded their skin and he couldn't determine left from right, under from over. All he knew, all he understood, was *her*.

And then she took the lead, setting him afire with hands that elicited gentleness and strength and sensitized his skin. She kissed his torso, worked her way down, down…

His body quivered at her initial touch.

"Shh," she soothed, nearly levitating him off the bed.

When she was done, when they both panted and their hearts pounded, she prepared him, and he cupped her face and said, "I love you, Addie." Then he entered her slowly, gently, savoring the act, honoring her before she cried his name and he called hers, and he rode her hard and fast until they fell over the edge together.

Night enveloping them in its peace and silence, Addie lay spooned within Skip's arms under the warmth and softness of the covers. They had made love twice before finally falling asleep, but at two o'clock she had woken from a dream she couldn't remember.

He shifted, brushing his chest hair along her spine. She smiled. She loved the hard contours of his body, the excess hair, the big, bony feet that hung over the end of the bed.

Tonight she had done things for the first time.

Again she smiled. Skip had loved her well. For so many years her bed had been a lonely place, sex with Dempsey automated and mechanical. Tonight Skip made her laugh and enjoy the moment. He'd been gentle when she wanted, urgent when she asked. Most of all, he'd let her choose.

Come morning she would catalog the marks of his lovemaking where he'd kissed her a little too fiercely. And she would glory in those prizes.

She couldn't imagine living without him again.

"Marry me, Addie," he whispered into her hair.

Her heart kicked. "You're awake."

He leaned over her shoulder. "Make a home with me. For Becky and Michaela."

Oh, God. He was offering what she had dreamed at seventeen. She said, "We need to tell the girls first." *About me.*

"We'll do it tomorrow." He set his mouth on her cheek. "There's no point in waiting."

"She really loved Hedy." *Becky.*

"She'll love you, too, honey." He stroked her arm.

"I don't know… It might be too soon."

He settled behind her again, pushed aside her hair and kissed her nape. "It'll be okay. We'll take it a day at a time."

Together. She liked the sound of that, liked the idea of Skip at her back, the way he was this moment.

Tucking his hand to her breast, she snuggled closer, and felt his body stir, strengthen. Thirteen years meant a lot of missed times. She pressed back, signaling.

"Again?" he asked, a smile in his voice.

"I want you, Skip."

"You have me, honey. Forever. And in case you're wondering, I'm clean—which I should've told you right away. I went through the tests when I decided to find Becky."

"For me it's been you and Dempsey."

"He was faithful?"

"He had faults, but infidelity wasn't one."

"I'm glad." And then he kissed her again. And again. Until the only sounds in the night were the rustling of sheets and the creaking of the bed.

Michaela bounded into Kat's kitchen and flung her arms around Addie's waist. "Mommy! We had fun! Aunty Kat let us make cookies and watch movies 'til really late, and me 'n' Becky 'n' Blake went swimming and Blake says I can dive really good now."

"Wow, that's fantastic, button." Smiling down at her daughter, Addie brushed the hair from her eyes. Beside Skip, Becky stood with her knapsack. His hand rested on her shoulder. Addie offered her a grin. "You girls ready to go home?" she asked.

"Uh-huh." Michaela bobbed her head. "'Bye, Blake. 'Bye, Aunty Kat."

"Thanks for everything," Becky said politely.

Kat saw them out the door. "See you soon, girls." Hugging

Addie, she whispered, "You're glowing." With a wink and a wave, she went back into the house and shut the door.

Addie couldn't ignore the warmth slipping across her cheeks. She and Skip…

They'd gotten perhaps four hours of sleep last night and her body felt the pleasant ache of unused muscles. This morning's bathroom mirror had reflected his kisses on her skin, and her marks on his. Wrapped in towels, they'd eaten omelets at seven, before donning jeans and short-sleeved shirts and driving to Kat's B and B.

"Where's your new t-t-truck, Mom?" Michaela asked as they climbed into Skip's Prius. "Is it nice? What c-c-color is it?"

"Green and it's very nice, you'll see once we're home," Addie said, noting Michaela's stutter had returned.

Because of Skip's presence?

She tried not to think how her relationship to Becky would affect Michaela, but she and Skip had planned to tell the children the moment they got home. As he turned onto Shore Road, he flashed her a quirky smile, one that understood her worries and said they were in this together. But with each passing mile, Addie felt the weight of their goal push her deeper into the seat.

Eight silent minutes later, they turned into Skip's lane and drove to the big white house with its turret and wraparound porch.

The girls trailed Addie inside.

"Aren't we going home, Mommy?" Michaela wanted to know.

"Not for a few minutes, hon." She smiled brightly. "First, we have something to tell you both."

Becky's eyes were wary, had been since Addie and Skip entered Kat's kitchen together. Now the girl looked from one adult to the other and said, "Come on, Mick. Help me put my stuff away." Whispering together, they ran up the stairs.

Addie followed Skip's broad, blue-shirted back into the kitchen where he started a pot of coffee.

A shiver cruised her skin. "I'm not sure this is the right time, Skip." Hugging her waist, she wandered to the glass patio-doors.

He came to stand behind her. "There's never going to be a right time." Cupping her shoulders, he brought her against his chest.

After a couple of seconds, Addie stepped away. "She's going to think we've conspired against her."

"How so?"

"We've been gone a day *and* a night."

"We explained why."

"The truck and house, I know. But I should've gone back to Kat's last night." Addie rubbed her arms. "Kids are incredibly astute. Did you notice how quiet Becky was in the car and—" she glanced at the ceiling "—just now?"

"They've had a lot of excitement in the past twenty-four hours."

Restless, Addie wandered the kitchen. "I have a bad feeling about this. It's too soon."

"Babe—"

Michaela ran into the room, her dark eyes wide and on Addie. "B-B-Becky s-s-says you're g-g-getting m-m-married!"

Skip darted a look at Becky. He hadn't expected his daughter to come to the marriage conclusion. At least not yet. What had Addie just said? *Kids are incredibly astute.* Stepping forward, he nodded to the kitchen table. "Why don't you girls sit for a minute?"

"Is it true?" Becky's gaze zipped between him and Addie.

With his own sudden misgivings—maybe Addie was right, they should wait—he drew out a chair for the woman his daughter eyed with a newfound caginess. "That isn't what this conversation is about, Bean. Come." He motioned her forward. "Sit down."

Michaela slid onto a chair adjacent to Addie, while Becky took the one next to him, which put her across the table from Addie, and Michaela opposite Skip.

"Girls," he began, glancing at Addie. From somewhere she'd

found the smile he didn't feel. "You both know Addie and I grew up on Firewood Island, right?"

"Yup." Michaela nodded enthusiastically. "Mommy w-w-went to the same s-s-school I did." Unaware of what was in store, she grinned at Becky. "And the same school where you'll go next week."

"Right," Skip said. "Which means we've known each other since we were little."

"S-s-small as me?" Michaela wanted to know.

"Almost," Addie said. Her eyes went from Michaela to Becky. "Your dad was two years older, so we really didn't become best friends until high school."

Becky's eyes remained riveted on Addie's face. Skip curled his hand gently around their daughter's forearm. "We became more than best friends. Addie became my girlfriend and I was her boyfriend."

"Eww! I'm never having a b-b-boyfriend." Michaela pulled a face that drew a chuckle from Skip—until he sneaked a peek at Becky.

Her face had gone egg-pale.

His heart thumped hard.

She knows, he thought. *She knows where this is going.*

"Becky," Addie said softly, reaching across the table.

The girl's mouth quivered. "You're...*her.*"

"Yes," Addie said.

"What, Mommy?" Bewildered, Michaela looked from one to the other. "Who's her?"

Becky turned and stared at Michaela, dazed perhaps to see the child on the next chair. Then her head turned and she looked at Skip. His heart plummeted when her bottom lip wobbled. Finally, her gaze settled on Addie. "Why?" Tears clouded her blue eyes. "Why didn't you want me?"

Michaela's brows bunched. "Mommy, why's B-B-Becky c-c-crying? Who d-d-didn't w-want you, B-Becky?"

"Bean," Skip said, needing to correct the child's mistake. "Addie wanted you very much."

A tear dripped to Becky's cheek and it was all he could do not to haul her onto his lap and hold her forever.

"I don't believe you," she said. "Either of you." Scraping back her chair, she jumped up and ran from the kitchen.

"Becky!" Michaela leaped up. "Wait!" Two seconds later, her feet thundered up the stairs after the older girl.

Addie set her fingers against her mouth and stared at the empty doorway. "I have to go to her." She pushed away from the table.

Skip caught her hand. Her skin was cold. "No. I was the one who started this whole damned thing." *Years ago, when I walked away from you.* "Let me finish it." *Fix it.*

Addie tugged her hand away. "It's me she holds responsible, Skip. It's me who needs her acceptance."

"You heard her. She blames us both."

She shook her head, her hair swaying along her shoulders. "Please. I know you want to intercede and make it all better, but I was the one who signed the papers."

His heart pinched. "Because of me."

"Because I made the choice."

"I won't let you take this on your own, Addie. I *caused* your decision. I'm not blameless, you know."

"No," she said, eyes somber. "You're not, but I still need to do this on my own, no matter the outcome." With that, she walked from the room.

Distress pounding through his veins, Skip clenched his fists. What the hell had he done? He should've listened to Addie, waited until he was sure Becky loved her, sure his daughter could not reject her mother for any reason. He should've waited until the bond between them had locked and the key tossed away—and nothing, *not one word,* could break it open.

* * *

Upstairs, Addie approached Becky's bedroom. The door was closed, but not shut. Through the three-inch gap—and the dresser mirror—she had a clear view of what was taking place. Becky sat on the bed, Michaela on her knees beside her, little arms wrapped around the girl's neck. They were whispering and rocking back and forth.

Heart ravaging her rib cage, Addie knocked softly.

The whispering persisted.

She knocked again, louder this time.

Becky checked the door before her gaze swung to the mirror and connected with Addie. The girl looked away.

Cautiously, Addie stepped inside the room. Hands pressed behind her back, she leaned against the wall beside the door, not daring to come closer.

Michaela looked at her mother. "Is Becky my sister, Mom?"

"Yes, honey. She is."

"Why didn't you want her?" Disquiet and anger wove through her girlish voice.

"I did, Michaela. I wanted Becky more than anything in the world."

"More than me?"

"Oh, sweet pea. You weren't born yet. I didn't know you when Becky was born."

"Then how come you sent her away?"

"I was very young and still in high school. I didn't think I could give her the home I wanted for her. I didn't think I could give her everything a little girl should have."

"Like Barbies?"

Addie's heart rolled over slowly. "Yes, like Barbies."

"But you gave them to me."

"When you were born, I was an adult. I was married to your father. I had a career. When I was in high school, I had nothing. I still lived with Grandma Charmaine."

Addie willed Becky to look at her—*please*—but the girl continued staring at the hooked rug beside her bed where bold mosaic patterns seemed to enclose the secrets of the earth.

Michaela said, "Becky's sad, Mommy. She thinks you didn't love her, but I told her you did."

"Oh, baby." The tears came fast and furious and Addie swiped at them with shaky hands. "I loved her so much. More than my own life. When I let the nurse take her away, I thought my heart had been ripped out of my chest. I wanted to die," she whispered.

Michaela looked concerned. "I don't want you to die, Mommy. I want Becky to be my sister and live with us."

Addie tried to smile. "I want that, too, but she lives with Skip and that's good because he's her father."

"Her real father," Michaela reasoned.

"Yes."

"Like you're her real mother?"

"Yes."

At that Becky broke her silence. "I already have a mom," she retorted without looking up.

"But she's—" Michaela began and Addie quickly held a finger to her lips. *Shhh.*

"Hedy was a wonderful mom," Addie said, thankful for this tiny inroad to speak to Becky. "I'm so glad she was in your life." *With all my heart, I wish I could bring her back for you.*

"She gave me everything," the girl went on, still not acknowledging Addie. "I loved her." She raised her head and looked at the photograph of a laughing, light-haired woman in a wooden frame on her night table. "I miss her." Her voice came as if from a great distance.

"I know you do, honey," Addie said. "And I never want to take away your love for her. I will never want to replace her in your heart, Becky. She is and always will be your mother."

Michaela said, "But you'll be sort of her mom, right?"

"Only if Becky wants that," Addie said, but the girl's attention was back to the rug and its vibrant blocks of color.

Addie struggled not to walk across the room, not to enfold both children in her arms. Years ago, she thought her heart had split into a trillion segments. But, here in this room, watching her child's grief and anger, her sense of rejection…

Addie's soul lay in shreds at her feet.

Chapter Thirteen

From the desk drawer Becky removed her diary. Outside the bedroom window sunshine sparkled on the leaves, turning them into gold and making the trees look as if they were dressed for a celebrity event.

Today had been a celebrity event for her.

Addie Malloy was her biological mother.

But hadn't she known way down deep? Hadn't there been something different about Addie? Something Becky couldn't quite reach, couldn't quite touch?

Her eyes burned. *Oh, man.* What would her mom think? What would she say? How would Hedy feel about Addie?

Brushing at her tears, she smoothed back the diary's next fresh page.

Mommy, I miss you soooo much. Please tell me every-thing is going to be all right. Show me in some way that you're still with me. I think of you every day. I miss you every day. I don't know what to think about Addie. How should I feel? I don't want her to take your place. She gave me away. You NEVER gave me away. You died trying to keep me safe. Addie said she never wanted to adopt me to anyone. She wanted to keep me. Then why didn't she? Oh, Mommy. I'm so confused so confused so confused. I hate feeling this way, THIS WAY.

She shut the diary. Her nose prickled. When she couldn't hold back anymore, she put her face in her arms over top of the book and cried.

School started four days later, on a clear and sunny day that belied the pounding of Addie's heart as she walked to her classroom. Thinking of Becky and Skip within the walls of the school, she had taken extra care with her makeup and appearance this morning and worn her favorite denim skirt and light-knit green top.

Throughout the day she would teach ninth- and eleventh-grade math, though her final block consisted of twenty seventh-graders. She knew without checking her attendance roster that Becky was in that final block.

Writing the upcoming homework assignments on the sideboard, she wondered if Skip had made the right choice upon registration. Maybe he should have put Becky in Lisa Wallace's math class.

And maybe, Addie thought, she and Skip should not have told the girl. Maybe they should've waited for a later date. A much later date.

Oh, face it. Later would still be too soon. No matter how many weeks and months went by—and regardless of how tight the bond between her and Becky—the right time, in Addie's mind, would never be justified. Such were the logistics of the matter.

Except, there was nothing logical—her dad's word—about telling a child you gave her away at birth.

Like an unwanted gift.

The thought broke the chalk between Addie's fingers.

No! No and no.

Becky had been very wanted. From the moment Addie realized she was pregnant, she had wanted the baby. Yes, she had cried and worried about her future and how she would raise her child, but she had never *not* wanted the baby, nor had she considered terminating the pregnancy.

Before leaving Becky's bedroom last Saturday morning, Addie tried to impress that wanting over and over. Sadly though, the girl hadn't seemed convinced. She'd ignored Addie until she left the room and went home. An hour later Skip brought Michaela to the house, and Addie spent the remainder of the weekend—between house repairs and Charmaine and Lee's questions, trying to explain the situation to her youngest child.

She had not seen Skip or Becky since, and the lack of that connection worried Addie.

To further her reservations, Michaela's stuttering returned fivefold, reminding Addie of the years when Dempsey lived with them. The child whined about wanting to see Becky, to call her, to visit the Dalton house, until late last night, after she knew the girls were in bed, Addie phoned Skip.

"How's it going?" she'd asked without preamble.

"Going," he said. He sounded tired. And crushed. "I didn't think she would take it this hard. She's barely come out of her room all weekend." He sighed. "When I found her, she wasn't this defiant."

"When you found her, she'd been in four foster homes, Skip. She was ready for a real home. I've seen it at school. Kids leaving long-term foster care are so ready for permanence and stability *they* do the adapting—even when it's back with their own parents. They'll do anything to make it work."

"Then why didn't she latch on to you?"

"Because she's had time to adjust, time to make *you* hers, so to speak. You've given her a feeling of security, and that security allows her to express her hurt and anger elsewhere. Which is a credit to what a great father you are. She feels secure enough in you, in not losing you, to take out her anger on me."

"Doesn't make me feel better," he grumbled.

"Bear with her. I'm betting she's bottled up a lot of Jesse's actions and behaviors, and now, after all is said and done, the woman who tossed her aside shows up and wants her back."

He was quiet for an extended moment. "You didn't toss her aside."

She pinched the bridge of her nose. "To her I did. Think of it, Skip. How would you perceive your mother had she given you up and then waltzed back into your life at a later date?" He had told her of Miriam's comments during their night together, of his parents reliving their own situation when Addie became pregnant.

"Hell. I don't know how I'd feel. Guys are different."

"But wouldn't you feel a sense of abandonment?" she stressed. "Of being unloved by your biological mother?" Addie's voice wavered. "Wouldn't you be terrified and angry?"

"Maybe. Guess it would depend on my life with the adopted parents. Most are incredibly loving, Addie."

She sighed. "I know. This is so damned hard."

"Aw, honey. Look, Friday after school I'm taking her to see my mom. Maybe getting to know other family members will help the transition."

Although he couldn't see her, Addie let a smile evolve. "Becky needs family so much. Once things settle, I'd like her to meet Lee and my mother, as well."

"She really likes Kat."

"Did she say that?"

"Yeah. At supper tonight. Out of the blue, she said she liked Kat's house and thinks Blake's cute."

"Typical girl."

"Yeah." His voice held a grin. "I had to remind her he was her cousin."

"What did she say to that?"

"Cool." Pause. "She said she's never had cousins or siblings. You know she's goofy over Michaela."

"And vice versa. My daughter called me selfish tonight because I haven't let her call Becky."

"Why haven't you?" Skip asked.

"I wasn't sure if she would want…either of us after… God. I've done it again, haven't I?"

"Done what?"

"Failed her. Even in this."

"Addie, you didn't fail her. You're giving her time. I'll tell her she can call Michaela tomorrow. How's that?"

Her heart rolled over. "Thank you."

The line was quiet for a few moments. Skip said, "She told me tonight that she'd suspected you were her mother from the day we met you at the library."

"Oh?"

"After we got our books and you'd already left, she asked me if there was something between us. She suspected we didn't like each other, if there was something in our past." He let out a soft laugh. "Smart kid."

"And then some. She questioned me about you the day her and Michaela helped extract honey."

He chuckled. "No grass growing under her feet."

They had talked a few more minutes, reassuring each other the days ahead would become easier. Addie hadn't slept well for the past three nights.

Now she set down the chalk and faced her first group of students with a smile. However, by the time the final block filed into her classroom, her nerves hummed like a hive of stressed bees.

Becky slipped into a desk at the back, her eyes glued on her books and binder as if she were gleaning spellbinding artifacts. A navy hoodie was pulled over her dark hair.

Addie began the lesson, reviewing the concept of decimal fractions and keeping the students on task by circulating the room, asking questions, noting answers and demanding tidy work.

She passed Becky's desk several times, and saw her daughter grasped the concept eagerly and wrote in a clean, precise hand.

On her last rotation around the room, she brushed the girl's shoulder, and whispered, "Excellent work," as she would to any student.

When the final bell rang, kids scrambled with homework and binders and pushed out the door into the hallway.

Packing up her work, Becky lingered. The hoodie had slipped from her hair as she lifted her knapsack onto her shoulder and gazed across the empty desks.

Addie tried to smile. "You like math."

Becky remained by her desk, unmoving. "How do you know?"

Because I loved it. "Because you were the first to remember the concept. And you're meticulous in your work."

The girl raised her chin. "My mom taught me that working neatly causes less errors."

My mom. Hedy. The barb struck hard. The child was determined to make a point. Addie's smile felt brittle. "Then we think alike."

Becky moved up between the rows. "No," she said, when she reached the front desk. "You don't think alike at all. She wanted me. You didn't." She turned and walked out of the room.

Lee called at four-thirty and said not to bother with supper, that she would be there in an hour with a chicken potpie. Before Addie could say a word the phone hummed. No sense in calling Lee back and telling her to forget it, Addie knew. The potpie was a ruse to discuss what her mother and sisters had no doubt burned up the phone lines about all weekend.

True to her word Lee arrived at five-thirty, impeccably attired as always, in a pair of trim black slacks and print top. Hugs, kisses and a discussion of Barbies were exchanged between Aunty Lee and Michaela before the girl returned to the living room where blankets, books and cushions were set up in tent fashion between chairs, sofa and coffee table.

Carrying the potpie, Addie led Lee into the kitchen.

"That's still hot." Her sister nodded to the dish. "Put it on the warmer if you're planning to make a salad or whatever."

Addie clicked on the warming burner. "I am." Turning to face her sister, she asked quietly, "Are you here to criticize me about Skip, Lee?"

The older woman cast a glance toward the kitchen doorway. "Hardly. But I can't believe you haven't said a thing to me about Becky, my *niece*," she whispered. An expression of hurt darkened her green eyes. "Kat's known for days."

"Oh, Lee... Kat guessed." Addie bowed her head and rubbed her forehead. Raising her eyes, she looked squarely at her sister. "I wanted to explain, but so much has happened, I just...couldn't get into it all again. You know how Mom is."

"I'm not Mom." Lee walked the ten feet between them. "It hurt, you know. It hurt that you wouldn't trust me with this. You're right, I thought Skip was the scum of the earth, but *this,* Addie... How could you believe I'd think anything but the best for you?" Tears stood in her eyes.

"How could I not?" Addie's voice squeaked. "You told me once that you planned to make sure Skip never fathered another child, that you'd wait, catch him unawares and then... Lee, you were so fierce about it. I really believed you were biding your time, that you had a bunch of bad-assed guys standing in the wings, waiting for your call." She breathed hard. "You were always so passionate when it came to family."

Lee's shoulders slumped slightly. She drew Addie into a hug. "You dummy. Don't you know I love you? I'd never hurt you, no matter what I said about Skip. I knew you loved him, that you've always loved the guy. Haven't you figured by now that I'm all bark and no bite?"

Addie laughed and wiped her wet eyes. "Well, that's not entirely true. You did slug Dempsey in the jaw when he moved out on me and Michaela."

"And broke my thumb in the process."

Addie took her sister's hand, kissed the crooked thumb in question. "He wasn't worth the pain you endured but, God, I was proud of you." She smiled into Lee's eyes. "You're my avenging angel, know that?"

Frowning, her sister stepped away. "Someone had to be."

Addie sighed. "Meaning Mom wasn't."

Lee snorted. "Have you forgotten what she said when Dempsey left?"

"All too well. He needed time to come to his senses."

"And has the bastard paid any alimony yet?"

"No."

Lee raised a lovely auburn eyebrow. "Want to argue the avenging angel further?"

Addie chuckled. "No, darlin'. But neither do I want you slugging my ex again should he show up in Burnt Bend in the future."

"Just as long as he doesn't come near you or Michaela. Don't ask me why, but somehow I would've preferred Skip over the dud whose name she carries."

Addie tucked her arms against her middle. "Skip may become her father, anyway. He's asked me to marry him."

Lee's smile was slow to evolve. "Well, now. Cancel all I've said about the man."

"Don't get your hopes up." Addie glanced toward the kitchen doorway. "Right now, Becky sees me as the interloper." Suddenly, the burn in her eyes intensified. "Sometimes, I wish…I wish he hadn't come back to the island, Lee. She was so happy with him before all this damn *stuff* came out of the woodwork."

Her sister cupped her shoulders. "Now you're just talking silly. Kat said Becky has a kind disposition and you know she wouldn't say something like that if she didn't feel it in her bones. Becky will come around. She won't be able to help it because she's just like you. She feels too much."

"Kat said that?"

"No, I'm saying it."

"But you haven't met her yet."

"I know her mother," Lee said, as if that said it all. "Now, let's get supper on the table before all of us evaporate with hunger."

Wednesday after school was football practice. Skip had arranged for Becky to go home with Addie, but the girl refused. She would rather sit through two hours of field practice while the team went through a series of drill circuits than be in Addie's company. Though she hadn't uttered exactly those words, the message was implied just the same.

So there his child sat, a small forlorn figure in her blue jacket, jeans and white sneakers; the coat's hood shielding her head, her nose buried in a book.

Skip frowned. He wasn't sure if she was hiding from him, the team or the world in general. He was, however, aware that in the two days she had attended school she had yet to mention Addie's name. He knew they saw each other in the hallways and in class. Hell, with a total enrollment of 318 and only two floors in the forty-year-old brick building, *everyone* saw each other at one time or another during the day.

He didn't dare ask how she liked Addie as a teacher. That would open a door he couldn't close, a door no doubt concealing anger and regret. Anger he could understand, but he hated the idea of Becky regretting Addie.

Once more he shot a look at the bleachers. Becky stared back, unsmiling. She didn't wave, didn't acknowledge that across the width of the field he recognized the sorrow in her blue eyes.

Dammit. How long would distress be their shadow? How long before she'd talk to him, really talk and laugh again? They'd come such a damn long way in the past ten months.

Veering his attention back to the team and its quarterback, Skip blew his whistle. *Get on with the practice, man. These kids are relying on you.*

But so was the girl sitting in the stands. Except with her, there was no practice, no game.

Only hard-core reality.

Friday evening Becky sat silent in the car while her dad drove toward town where they would have supper at her Grandmother Dalton's house.

Becky was excited *and* scared. She'd never had a real grandma before. Hedy and Jesse's parents died before she'd been born. Now, not only did she have parents again, she had an aunty and a grandma. Two of each, really—if she counted Addie's mom and other sister in Burnt Bend.

Addie...

Oh, boy. Becky so wanted to talk to her dad and tell him all the things jammed in her head about her math teacher...and biological mother. In class, every time the woman walked past Becky's desk, her heart would pound so hard she was sure her T-shirt moved.

She wished all this confusion would just go away. She couldn't stop thinking about Addie—or about Hedy.

She couldn't stop comparing the two women. She hated that she compared. Hedy was her *mother.*

But so was Addie. Hard as Becky tried, she could not stop liking her biological mother. Ever since she had shown her the bees and explained how honey got into the stores, she had liked her.

Then there was the nightmare at Ms. O'Brien's place. Like Hedy, Addie had come to her side immediately, calmed her, talked things through so she could fall back asleep. Addie promised to show her how to bake bread to help with her memories of Hedy.

And Michaela. *Omigod.* A little sister! How cool was that? Becky knew without a doubt she already loved Mick.

The kid was cute and smart and fun. At seven years old she could talk about stuff like the environment and the way kids in Africa were dying of disease and starvation. Which totally blew Becky away. Even her best friend Kirsten hadn't talked about those kinds of issues, and Becky often wished she had, because they were important. But whenever Becky mentioned a TV documentary, Kirsten would whine, *Let's not talk about boring stuff.*

Sometimes she didn't miss Kirsten at all. And that was kind of scary. Oh, they still e-mailed every day, but in the past few weeks Becky had gotten tired of Kirsten's same old stories about how boring summer was and how stupid the boys were and who was wearing what and who was out of the group she used to hang with.

At Fire High she had hooked up with a couple girls in the "fast" math club Addie organized a couple days ago. At first, Becky hadn't wanted to join, because it would mean seeing Addie after school twice a week in addition to class. But the girls had begged Becky.

You're way smart, Jillian, the girl sitting in the next row said yesterday. *And it's only for kids that love math and want more of a challenge. C'mon, it'll be fun.* So she'd signed up.

"We're here," her dad said, breaking into her thoughts as he pulled into the treed driveway leading to a brown house with a green roof and a front porch.

A black-and-white dog climbed slowly to its feet and, wagging its feathery tail, ambled down the steps.

"Hey, old girl," her dad greeted the dog when he got out of the car. "Good to see you're still kicking around. Bean, come meet Splashes." He bent to gently scratch the dog's furry chest. "When I was seventeen, she was a little puppy."

"Wow," Becky said, amazed. "That means she's a hundred and twelve in dog years."

The front door opened and a tall, slim woman dressed in black pants and a pink blouse stepped onto the porch. Becky could see where her dad got his dark hair and brown eyes.

"So," she said, waiting for them to come up the stairs. "This is my granddaughter. Hello, dear." She took Becky's hands. Mrs. Dalton's skin was cool, as if she was anxious. Becky relaxed a little. "I'm so glad you're here," Mrs. Dalton said, offering a cheek to her son. "Skip."

"Mom." After kissing the woman's cheek, he set a hand on Becky's shoulder. "Is that roast chicken I smell?"

Mrs. Dalton grinned. "You thought I'd forget your favorite dish?" She winked at Becky. "Come in."

Becky liked Mrs. Dalton. She liked the way the woman moved her long, slender ballerina hands when she talked.

The house was fancy in an old-fashioned way, and both the front and backyards looked like Japanese rock gardens Becky had seen in one of her mom's magazines. No flowers or bees in sight.

After dinner, they sat in wicker chairs on the back deck. The evening was warm and Becky was petting Splashes when Mrs. Dalton said she could call her Miriam. Except it didn't feel right. The woman was her dad's mom and she had wrinkles around her eyes.

"Can I call you Grandma instead?" she asked.

"Sure, dear." Mrs. Dalton smiled at Becky's dad. "Son, could you get us the dessert? It's the apple crisp in the fridge. And we'd like it à la mode."

The second the door closed behind her dad, Mrs. Dalton's

smile disappeared. She said, "I wanted a moment alone with you."

Becky's throat suddenly squeezed shut. Was Mrs. Dalton mad?

The woman twirled a diamond ring on her finger. "Every day I thought about you and prayed you were okay." Her eyes went watery. "And now you're here with your daddy. I can barely believe it."

"Me, neither."

"I hope we can get to know each other."

"I want to know everyone," Becky said. In her heart she knew that included Addie.

"And you will," her grandmother said. "Give it time." She smiled a sad smile. "Can you do an old woman a favor?"

Becky shrugged. "Sure."

"Please don't hold the past against your parents."

Beck said nothing. She figured her grandmother meant Addie.

"They were very much in love, you see, and wanted to marry."

That startled Becky. "Then why didn't they?"

Mrs. Dalton's head shook a little. "Let's not dwell on the past, child. It does nothing but eat at your insides."

Petting Splashes, Becky felt her eyes sting. "I had a great mom."

"Yes, darling, you did, and for that I'm indebted." Suddenly she leaned forward and patted Becky's knee. "Listen, would you like to go shopping with me one Saturday after you've settled in with school? Maybe we could get your other grandma to bring little Michaela."

"Really?" The rock on Becky's heart tumbled away.

"Of course." Grandma Dalton smiled. "We'll go to Seattle, shop for some pretty clothes, eat hot-fudge sundaes for lunch and take in a movie. What do you say?"

"Cool. I mean, that would be nice. I never had a sister to shop with. Or a grandma," Becky added shyly.

"Then it's a date. I'll arrange everything."

At that moment Becky's dad returned with three steaming desserts on a tray. As they ate, she listened to Mrs. Dalton tell him about the shopping plans, and watched his eyes fill with happiness.

Wow. Her parents, her *real* parents, had wanted to marry each other. They'd wanted her after all.

Addie had wanted her.

Becky felt like dancing—and crying. Because of Hedy. Because of the mother she'd loved with all her heart.

She had to set things right, and there was only one way to do it.

Next week couldn't get here fast enough.

Chapter Fourteen

At ten on Saturday morning Charmaine knocked on Addie's front door.

"Mom," she said, surprised. Charmaine always called before driving "out to the country," as she liked to refer to the home Addie had made of her grandparents' place. Both Kat and Lee lived in town, no more than a two-minute drive from each other and Charmaine.

Her mother strode inside. "When were you going to tell me?"

About Becky. First Lee, now their mother. Addie followed Charmaine to the kitchen. "Today, actually."

Charmaine grabbed a mug from the cupboard and helped herself to the coffeepot. "This fresh?"

"Five minutes ago." Addie stood in the doorway, hands in the pockets of her hoodie. "If you've come to rant, Mom—"

"'Course I've come to rant. I'm hurt, that's what. You told Kat and Lee and they've known *for a week!* How *could* you not tell me that I have another granddaughter?"

"You've always known about your first granddaughter," Addie stated calmly, tamping down her ire. Charmaine was part of the package that convinced Addie at seventeen to "do what's right."

"I mean, living here, Addie," Charmaine said. "In the same town."

"She lives out of town."

Her mother waved a hand. "Semantics. So why didn't you tell me? By the way, where's Michaela?"

"With Becky."

"Is that her name?" Her mother pursed her lips. "Short for Rebecca? Not sure I like it."

Addie pushed away from the doorframe, went to pour her own coffee. "Too late. It's the name her mother gave her and *I* like it."

"*You're* her mother."

"Semantics. Did you know the name means joined?"

"Joined?" Charmaine frowned. "What's that got to do with anything?"

Addie shook her head. "Nothing." But it did. After Becky revealed the definition of Hedy's name, Addie had looked up Rebecca, and could see why Hedy selected the name. Following years of wanting a baby, she had been *joined* with one at last.

"So when do I get to see her?" Charmaine wanted to know.

"When I think it's right." Addie checked the five rounds of dough she had set to rise on the counter before breakfast, before Michaela had crept out of bed, sleepy-eyed and wanting a snuggle. Addie smiled at the memory. Her baby. Would the day come when Becky also needed a snuggle?

Charmaine sat at the kitchen table. "Why are you putting me on hold? Kat's already seen her, and so has Lee."

"Lee hasn't. And Kat saw her because she watched the girls when I went to Seattle."

"Oh, yes. About Seattle. I heard you spent the whole day

with Skip Dalton. Are you two getting back together for the sake of the girl?"

A headache niggled at the base of Addie's skull. "Her name is Becky, Mom. And, no, we aren't getting back together for her sake. If wc do, it'll be because *we* want to."

Charmaine's eyes narrowed. "So you've discussed it?"

"Mom, this is really none of your business."

"It is when you ignore me over your sisters."

Addie wanted to scream. "I didn't ignore you! I stayed with Kat when a tree fell on my house." *Which is now repaired, thank you for asking.* "And Michaela asked if Becky could come, as well."

Her mother's eyebrows swung up. "Michaela's that close to her?"

"They've become like sisters." Addie tried to sound as pleased as she felt, but Charmaine's sharp scrutiny deflated her delight. Why did she always let her mother make her feel as though she had made a mess of her life? Looking away, she sipped her coffee.

Charmaine remained silent as she studied Addie. "Well," she said at last, "for Michaela's sake, I'm glad. The poor tyke has been through so much these past years, what with you taking over your father's bees and then moving out of town to this… farm."

"Mom, as much as it grates on you, Mick loves it here. She's happier than she's ever been. And—" Addie couldn't check her joy "—since hooking up with Becky, she hardly stutters any-more."

"Mick?" Charmaine focused on Addie's slip.

"It's a nickname Becky gave her." Without realizing it, Addie had let the word flow out as natural as honey from her extrac-tor.

"Sounds like a boy's name."

Suddenly annoyed, Addie gazed at Charmaine. "Don't make

this about you, Mother. Be happy for the girls, okay? They need each other. Especially now that Becky knows the whole story. She's been through hell, and is going through another avenue of it right this minute. I'm glad she has Michaela on her side. If she wants to call her Mick, so be it."

Charmaine blinked. "You don't need to yell, Adelina. I didn't mean anything by it."

"I'm not yelling, and yes, you meant every word. You're upset I didn't tell you right away. Truth is, I've had to do a bit of emotional adjusting, as well. So has Michaela."

Her mother reached to take Addie's hand. "I'm sorry, honey. You're right. I've been nursing a hurt about the whole thing since before school started. I kept wondering what I'd done that would cause you not to trust me with such crucial news."

Addie held her mother's gaze for a moment, then she went to the heated oven. "I didn't know if you'd be happy," she admitted, slipping on a pair of thick mitts.

"Why on earth wouldn't I be happy?"

"Because you didn't stop dad from convincing me to sign those adoption papers. You didn't say one word." Abruptly, the anger rushed back. "Why, Mom? Why didn't you support *me?*"

Charmaine's mouth twisted. Her shoulders sagged. "Oh, Addie. Your daddy was raised to believe that having babies out of wedlock wasn't right. That it was…"

"Scandalous."

"Yes. Archaic as it sounds." She drew in a long breath. "His parents were from the old country. When they started the bee-keeping business here, they were quite poor, barely able to clothe their kids. Your daddy couldn't finish school. Instead, he joined his daddy's bee business." Her shoulders rose on another sigh. "And then you came along, smart as a whip. He couldn't let you pass up your future."

Any more than Ross Dalton could let Skip pass up his NFL chance.

Addie wanted to claw at something. "So, instead, he passed up his grandchild."

Charmaine's eyes begged for understanding. "I tried to change his mind, truly I did, but he wouldn't listen. All he could think about was the opportunities you could have with your intelligence."

"He hated Skip," Addie said, remembering the outrage her father had toward Ross Dalton, Skip's father. An outrage she never understood.

"He hated that Skip came from money. That he was…"

"What?"

Charmaine shook her head. "Nothing. It no longer matters."

"Your face says it did matter, Mom. Spit it out."

"Oh, Addie, it's old news. Your father is dead. Let it go."

"Fine. But understand this. *I* will not give Becky up again. Not for anyone or anything. And I don't care who knows. I'm proud of my children, and who they've become." She lifted her chin. "If you have a problem with that you'd best leave now."

Charmaine rose from her chair and crossed the floor. "Oh, my dear girl." She enfolded Addie in a hug. "The only problem is waiting until I see my first grandchild. I wish with all my heart it could be this minute."

Addie breathed easier. "Okay. Maybe we can arrange for a meeting sometime next week. I'll ask Skip."

Her mother cupped her face. "I look forward to it." Then she set her forehead against Addie's and whispered, "I love you, baby. Can we please start over?"

Following the night he spent in Addie's bed ten days ago, Skip looked forward to their late-night calls like a lost man facing his first meal after a week in the wilderness. He craved the sound of her voice. He needed the electricity her whispered words sent through his blood. He ached for the touch of her hands, her mouth, her body.

In short, as a song once said, he *hungered* for her.

By unspoken agreement, they took turns calling; one night he'd pick up the phone, the next she'd dial his cell number. Cell phones that rang privately in their bedrooms without waking the house. Tonight was his turn.

Lying against his pillows, he checked to make sure it was ten-fifteen, *their time,* then pressed speed 2.

"Hey." Her voice held a smile when she answered.

"God, I miss you." They were almost finished the second week of school and had yet to retrieve a minute's worth of face time. "I need to hold you, Addie. Just to…*hold* you." Imagining, he closed his eyes.

"Soon," she said, and he heard a tide of longing in that single word. "How is she doing?"

Becky. He'd told Addie about dinner with his mother last Friday evening and, in turn, she described her Saturday session with Charmaine.

"Still hides in her room. Won't talk much past one-syllable words. But I see a glimmer of hope. I heard she's joined your three o'clock Tuesday-Thursday fast-math class."

"Yes. She's incredibly bright. Today was our first session and she's already into ninth-grade algebra."

"Last year the teacher had her slotted in advanced placement for both science and math. She's her mother's child clear through. Another Math-addical." He smiled, though she couldn't see him.

"Good heavens." Addie laughed quietly. "It's been years since I've heard that name. I'm amazed you remembered."

"When it comes to you, I remember everything."

"Well, that's one thing I want you to forget. I hated when people called me that. It was so…nerdish. Do you know how awful it is to be considered a nerd?"

"They envied you, Addie." Not only for her smarts, but because he—the school's star quarterback—showed interest in her, dated her. Loved her.

"Right, and look who had the last laugh. They did." She sighed. "Dammit, Skip, I'm sorry. That wasn't called for."

"It's all right. You can vent with me all you want. I'm not leaving. Ever." He heard her sheets rustle. Was she changing positions in bed? He wished he lay beside her.

She said, "I'm so antsy I can hardly think anymore. What if our little girl goes through the same sort of horridness?"

"Addie, you're trying to second-guess the future. Don't. Becky has something we didn't. Two parents who—barring she chooses some sort of illegal activity—will always support her decisions. We won't let her down. We'll make mistakes, undoubtedly. Parenting, I've discovered, is damned hard. But we'll be there for *her.*"

"Do you think she'll agree to us marrying one day?"

The question had his body humming. "God, I hope so. I want nothing more than to lie down with you every night of my life, and wake up to your sweet smile every morning. Addie…I love you so much. It's all I can do to not climb out of this bed and sprint to your house and put my hands on you."

A long pause ensued. "Why don't you?" she whispered.

Every molecule of blood thrummed. "Now, you mean?"

Again he heard the sheets shift—and a soft grunt. "I'll meet you halfway. Skip, I need to kiss you so badly."

He threw back the covers. "Babe, I'm there."

Naked, he strode to his dresser, grabbed out a pair of flannel gym pants and a long-sleeved Broncos sweatshirt.

At the far end of the hallway, he checked at Becky's door to make sure she slept. A soft snore drifted from her bed. Down the stairs he went, his heart booming in his chest. At the back door, he shoved his bare feet into his shabbiest sneakers and crept out of the house.

Ten trillion stars poked through the velvet backdrop of night, illuminating property and road. Off to the left, above the silhouetted trees, sailed a moon-boat.

Once he cleared the corner of the house, Skip ran as if the ghost of Reggie White chased him down the game field.

Approaching Addie's house, he slowed to a jog and attempted to regain his breath. Was she outside? Around back, on the stoop? He searched the night and, for an instant, felt defenseless against its obscurity.

"Over here," she called softly, and he spotted her in front of her new truck parked near the honey shed. Though the stars cast her in an array of shadows, the small pale shape of her face guided him to where she waited.

She stood in bare feet, dressed in dark yoga pants and a sweatshirt, and the instant he touched her, the second his arms hauled her against his chest and his mouth found hers, he knew she wore nothing beneath those two items. "Addie," he muttered, feasting on her taste. "God...Addie."

His hands dove under cloth and fabric, seeking warm skin and supple curves. She hooked a bare heel around his calf, pulling his hips closer. He turned her, a choreographer of dance, to press her against the hood of the vehicle. His fingers were in her hair, his teeth nipping the flesh in the V of her shirt.

And then her hand dove into the waist of his pants and found his nakedness, and he let out a deep groan. "Addie—*wait.*"

"No." Her breath seared his neck. "Here. Now."

"I don't have protection."

This time she groaned, and he pulled her against him, holding her face, kissing her mouth, kissing her hard. Before he could count to five, he settled them against the truck, urgency singing in his veins.

Addie, he thought, and could think no more.

By degrees the rush eased. Under her shirt where his hands traveled, and on her neck where his lips tarried, her skin burned with a fever that equaled his own. He remained surrounded by her, unwilling to break the union of arms and hands and mouths.

She whispered, "It's like we're teenagers again."

His hold tightened. "For you, my heart will always be young. I love you, Addie. I can't say it enough."

"Just say it every night before we go to sleep." She smiled against his jaw. "I want you in my dreams."

"I want you in my bed. Every night."

"Before you know it." She slipped from his embrace and the cool night air sent a shiver across his skin. Already he missed her.

One last kiss, then she stole through the shadows toward the rear of her house.

"Let's set a date," he called quietly. He hated sneaking around; hated life without both kids under one roof.

She hesitated, a foot on the lower step. Starlight shimmered in her hair. "Ask Becky, and I'll ask Michaela. We'll go from there." Then the door snicked shut and she was gone.

Riding a seesaw of emotion, he walked back to his house. If they had to steal around for a few more months until the girls felt comfortable with them both, he would do it without question.

"Dad?"

Skip's head snapped toward his front porch. "Becky?" She sat in her pajamas, huddled on the top step. "What're you doing out here?"

"I woke up and you weren't in the house." Fear traced her voice.

He walked over and climbed the steps to sit beside her, his arm brushing her shoulder. "I heard a noise," he said, knowing it was a lie, but also knowing he could not in this lifetime expose the truth. "So I went to check it out."

"What was it?"

He shrugged. "Probably raccoons, or a herd of deer." Then because he'd missed her presence this past week, he gave her an affectionate one-armed hug and kissed her hair. "Come on, Becky. Tomorrow's another school day."

They went through the front door, into the warmth of the

house. Upstairs, Skip tucked his daughter into bed. "Good night, Bean."

"'Night."

He was about to pull the door partially closed when she whispered, "Do you love her?"

He didn't need to ask whom. Returning slowly to the bed, he lowered himself to its edge. "I do, Becks. Very much."

"Are you going to marry her?"

"Would that be so terrible?"

She rolled away, presenting her back, curling into a fetal position. "I don't care what you do."

"But I care what you think," he replied, wishing he could see her face. His heart banged his chest. If they couldn't get past this, how would he and Addie have a life together? "And I'm hoping..." He had no idea how to say what he hoped. "That it'll work out for us all," he finished.

She stayed motionless and mute for so long he thought she'd fallen asleep, but then she said, "I might not go to school tomorrow."

"Oh?" Tension ran through his body. "Why's that?"

"I don't want to talk about it," she mumbled.

"Bean, if you're trying to get back at me for loving Addie, not going to school isn't going to work."

"Not everything is about her, y'know."

"Then what?" He leaned over to switch on the night lamp.

"Don't," she said, and he drew his hand back.

"What is it?" Worry spiked his pulse rate. "Are you feeling sick?"

"Sort of."

He waited for an explanation. Then it hit him. *She's a girl, dummy.* Breathing a little easier, he suggested, "How about we see what the morning brings?"

When she didn't respond, he said good-night again, rose and walked quietly out her door. Would he ever know all there was to raising a daughter? *Addie would.* Or at least she'd have a better inkling of these things than him.

In his bedroom, he lay staring through the dark and rehearsed a thousand ways to tell Becky he needed to include her mother to make his life and hers complete.

When dawn outlined the treetops with pink, Becky woke and got out of bed. She loved the sunrises here. In the trailer park, there hadn't been many sunrises because she'd been too tired most mornings after listening half the night to Jesse and her mom argue in the next room. She hadn't understood the words, but she had known they weren't good. Sometimes she heard her mom cry. She hated those nights most of all.

But here... Here there was peace and quiet in the mornings. And the sky and the trees were so pretty. She loved that she could open her window and hear the birds, so many different kinds of birds. And once, just after the sun went down, she'd seen deer step out of the forest to graze in the back yard. How cool was that?

This morning she sat at her desk, the one she and Skip— sometimes she still thought of him as Skip—had picked out before moving to Firewood Island. Today was her mom's birthday and she was writing her a letter.

Dearest Mom,
I miss you so much but I want you to know I'm okay.

Then she wrote about Skip, her dad. She knew her mom would be happy he was the one raising her, and not foster parents or another adopted family. She wanted Hedy to know all the wonderful things about her new home. The trees and birds and deer. The town and its library. Her new school and her dad's coaching abilities.

Becky wrote about Michaela—*Oh, Mom, I have a little*

sister!—and her Aunt Kat and Grandma Dalton, although it was sort of hard to think of Mrs. Dalton as Grandma, 'cause they'd only met once.

When she had written about everyone and everything, she reread her words and knew she still had the hardest part to write, the part about Addie.

No matter how guilty she felt, Becky knew she had to tell her mom. She had to get it all out. Because this would be her final letter to Hedy. After today, she had to put the past in the past.

With a deep breath, she began the last paragraph.

Mommy, you know I've met my real mom, Addie. Even though I'm still mixed up about her I honestly can't say she isn't nice. Because she is. She's really great with my little sister & she's the best teacher & I think Dad has loved her forever & she's loved him. Thing is, I'm starting to like her a lot, too. But I don't want you to think I'll love her more than you. In my heart you'll always be my mom. But I think she would like to be my mom, too & maybe one day that will be ok. I just want you to know that if it happens, it doesn't mean I've forgotten you. It just means that I'll have 2 moms who I love. One here and one in heaven. You know a few months ago I thought I'd never have a mom again. Now I have 2. That's kinda kewel, don't ya think? So, Mommy, I have to say goodbye. I have to let you go. I'll always think of you & love you but me & Mick want to be sisters & that means being a family with my dad & Addie. In my heart I know you'll be happy for us b/c that's the kind of mom you are. It's the kind of mom Addie is, too.

She read the words, and satisfied, signed the letter *Love forever, Becky,* before sealing the page into an envelope and putting it into her knapsack with the ferry tickets.

Chapter Fifteen

At ten-forty, Principal Holby and the vice principal came to Addie's door while she was teaching second block.

Holby motioned her into the hallway where he said, "The elementary school just phoned. Michaela didn't come in from recess. Was she supposed to leave the premises? Her teacher says there wasn't a note this morning stating otherwise."

Addie thought the floor would cave beneath her feet. "What do you mean, she didn't come in? She's there. I dropped her off almost two hours ago." Her voice rose as she fought hysteria.

Holby took her elbow, nodded to the vice principal. "Bill's going to take your eleventh graders. Let's go to the office and sort this out."

"Forget the office. I'm going to Mick's school." She broke into a run, calling over her shoulder, "Phone the police." *Michaela. Omigod. Michaela, where are you?*

She flung out of the main doors, her ankle twisting painfully with her high heels. Why had she worn a dress today? *Michaela...*

Hopping on one foot, then the other, she took off her shoes and raced in stocking feet down the sidewalk. The elementary school was a block away. As she ran, she checked her watch. Twelve minutes since the recess bell had brought the students back to class. Twelve minutes equaled how far?

Not far.

Very far in a car.

But not on an island, she reasoned, ignoring the pain the cement initiated on her bare heels. Except…there were twenty square miles of island. With two-thirds woods and rough hills and a semimountain.

Addie sprinted into the school's driveway.

Belle Sherman, the principal, and her assistant waited with Kat under the portico of the entrance doors.

"Addie!" Her sister rushed forward. "It's okay. She's with Lee."

"With…Lee?" Her heart thrashed, an untamed creature between her ribs. *Thank God, thank God.* "Why's she with Lee?"

"I don't know, but she phoned me, said I should get here immediately since I lived closest. Figured you'd be a mess. And she was right." Kat smiled. "Take a deep breath, honey. Anyway, they were down at the ferry dock. Becky and Michaela both. Belle called Skip."

Addie dropped her shoes and shoved her hands into her hair. "Oh, Kat. I thought I'd die on the spot when they told me she was…was…"

Her sister's arms surrounded Addie in a fierce hug. "It's over, sis. She's safe. They're both safe. Lee's driving them to the school right now." Easing her grip, she looked past Addie. "Someone's here."

"Addie." His deep voice spun her around. He stood a few feet away, the sun sharpening the hard angles of his face and deepening the brown of his eyes. His big hands flexed at his sides and his chest pumped under the expensive fabric of his tailored tan shirt as if he'd raced the distance like a receiver bent on a touchdown.

"Skip… Oh, God, Mick and Becky…" She gulped air. "Why would they run away?"

Oblivious of their audience, he came forward, kissed her forehead and wiped her cheeks with his thumbs. "We'll find out in a minute, sweetheart. First, we need to take care of your poor heels." And then he hoisted her into his arms and carried her inside to the medical room, where he tended to her torn feet.

When Lee's red Jeep turned the corner of the school's street, Addie covered her mouth and rolled her lips inward to hold back a cry. She could see the girls in the rear seat, eyes anxious.

The instant Lee stopped alongside the curb, the back door opened. Michaela hopped out first, then Becky.

"Michaela Jane," Addie began, anger overriding angst now that she knew the girls were safe. "What on earth were you thinking to leave school property when you did *not* have my permission to do so?"

Becky stepped forward. "It's my fault." She looked at Skip standing beside Addie. "I'm sorry, Daddy." Her voice was soft and full of tears. "Yesterday, I told Mick I was going to visit my mom's…my mom's grave…b-because today is her birthday. And…" She took Michaela's hand. "My…my little sister wanted to come and keep me company while I said…while I said—" she pushed a palm against her nose "—goodbye."

"Oh, little one," Addie murmured, taking a step toward the children.

"Bean." Skip hunkered down on the balls of his feet and Addie knew he was putting himself on a less threatening level. "Was this what you meant last night about being 'sort of' sick?"

Clearly distraught, the girl nodded. "I didn't mean to cause so much trouble. Guess I should've told you or…or left a note."

"You're right," Skip agreed. "Telling us would have been the right thing, the *only* thing to do."

A tear crept down her cheek and her chin wobbled. Addie

glanced at Skip. His Adam's apple shifted on a swallow as he reached for their daughter's hand.

"It's okay, Becky." Michaela hugged her sister. "Maybe Mommy and your daddy will take us to your mom's grave."

Oh, button, your heart is so big. Clasping Skip's shoulder, Addie said, "Mick's right, Becky. We'll take you there today."

"You will?" The girl stared at Addie.

"A birthday is just too important to miss."

Becky blinked back tears.

Addie spoke to Lee, who was waiting behind the wheel of her Jeep, elbow hooked on the windowsill. "Are you booked this afternoon?"

"Nope." She grinned. "Matter of fact, I'm free until four."

"Good. That'll give Skip and I—" she squeezed his shoulder "—time to call in a couple of substitute teachers for the afternoon, and the girls to gather their homework. Will that work for you and your team, Skip?"

He rose, knees popping. "The assistants can handle practice for one day. My family comes first." He turned to Lee and smiled. "Hey, Lee. It's been a while."

She nodded. "A tad."

"Thanks for bringing the girls."

"No problem. Just glad I was getting my morning java at Coffee Sense when I saw Michaela heading for the ferry ticket office."

"We owe you."

"They're my nieces. There's nothing to owe. So. Meet you all at my dock in about thirty minutes?"

"Sounds like a plan," Skip said gruffly.

Addie slipped her hand in his as Lee pulled from the curb. "Thanks," she mouthed to her sister.

Michaela jumped up and down. "Yippee! We get to fly in Aunty Lee's plane, Becky!"

"Hold on, pint," Skip said, crouching again. "Going in Aunty Lee's plane isn't a reward for what you girls did."

Immediately subdued, Michaela nodded. "I'm s-s-sorry, S-Skip. I'll never leave the s-s-school again."

He took her hand in his large one. "That's good, because you don't want Mom or me to cry."

Her eyes widened. "You'd cry?"

"If you or Bean were lost and we couldn't find you? Oh, honey, we'd cry to fill a lake."

Addie watched as her baby stepped forward, set her little palm against his jaw. "Please, don't cry, Skip. I don't like it when Mommy's sad."

Pulling her forward, he kissed her hair. "Okay," he whispered. "Only if you and Bean promise to always tell us your plans."

"We promise. Come on, Mom." Michaela tugged Addie toward the school doors. "Let's get my homework so Becky can fly in Aunty Lee's plane."

"All right." She chuckled. "I'm coming."

At the doors, she couldn't help one last look back at the man who, in a single moment, had become a father to her youngest child. Hand on Becky's shoulder, he walked toward the high school, their dark heads glimmering in the sun, their posture and gait so endearingly familiar.

And then Becky cast back a glance, too—and her shy smile shone into Addie's heart.

The flight to the mainland in Lee's red and white Cessna 185 took twenty minutes. While Lee remained at the small municipal terminal talking with several pilots, Skip rented a car and drove his girls to the cemetery.

His girls.

Yes, Addie, Becky and Michaela *were* his girls, his family now. In the rearview mirror, he watched the children, heads bent together, whispering girly things to each other. Beside him, Addie searched along the tree-lined street for the place that could heal their daughter…or send her into a darker place than she'd been four years ago.

The cemetery came into view and a balloon filled his throat. As he pulled into the small parking lot, the girls quieted. Turning in the seat, he asked, "Do you know where your mom is, Bean?"

Her blue eyes darted to Addie, and his heart jerked. "Yeah," she said. Gathering up her knapsack, she opened the car door. When they stood under the wrought iron sign over the bricked entranceway, she stared ahead, closed off from them once more. "I want to go alone, okay?"

Skip nodded. "We'll be right here in case you need us."

Head bent, she started up the pebbled path, a small lone figure against a field of bleached stone markers. His heart went with her.

Michaela stood between Addie and Skip, and suddenly her little fingers curled around his. Without looking down, without drawing attention to the gesture, he gently took her hand.

"She's saying goodbye," Michaela informed them as they watched Becky kneel on the grass at a distance of a hundred paces.

"Goodbye?" Addie looked down at her child.

"Uh-huh. She wrote her mom a letter and told her that she has to say goodbye 'cause she's gotta be with her other mom now." The child glanced up. "You, Mommy."

"She said that?" The leap of hope in Addie's eyes tore at Skip.

"Uh-huh," Michaela went on, watching Becky. "An' she wants me to be her real sister."

"But you are her real sister, button."

"No, I mean, that we gotta have the same last name."

"Really?" Addie's eyes flew to Skip and he swallowed hard.

"Uh-huh. She said so when we went to the ferry. She wants us to live in her house—I mean, in Skip's house—an' she wants me to have the bedroom next to hers, an' she wants me'n her to bake bread and cookies together, an'— Here she comes." Unable to wait any longer, Michaela ran forward, hands flapping little-girl style at her sides, down the path toward Becky.

"Omigod, Skip," Addie whispered when Becky clasped Michaela's hand. "Our baby is so strong, *so* strong."

"They both are, honey." Skip looked down into her eyes, misty with tears. "They're part of you."

Together they waited for the girls to walk through the gate. And for Becky to come home at last.

The scent of baked bread infused the house.

Humming to herself, Addie pulled out the last of four loaves from Skip's oven—though these days it was more her own—and turned each onto thick towels spread across the counter. Outside the wide windows the backyard lay awash in a gray October rain that had come with the dawn and had continued into the afternoon.

A perfect Saturday for baking, especially with the help she'd had in the process.

Addie smiled. When she'd promised several weeks ago to teach Becky about bread making, it was to grant the child a memory-coping technique. But this morning, with her instructions on how to mix the dough from scratch, knead it, separate it into rounds, cover it for rising...Addie discovered she'd passed on something else. She'd passed on an old and honored practice traveling back along the generations, grandmother to mother to daughter.

"Maybe one day," Becky had said, a patch of flour in her dark hair, "I can teach somebody to make bread."

"And how to keep bees," Michaela had volunteered.

And maybe one day they would. Maybe one day both traditions would pass on to *their* children.

Yes, Addie thought, much had changed since the day at the cemetery in Lynnwood. That day, Becky had accepted Addie, lifting the tension between them. Perhaps someday she would even say "Mom." But the word wasn't key to Addie's happiness. No, that revolved around Becky's love for Michaela and Skip.

"You're cheerful."

She glanced up. Phone in hand after a call to an assistant coach, he sat in the eating nook surrounded by rain-drenched windows. On a clear day they looked out on the nearby forest and its scattering of birdhouses.

"Care to share?" Skip asked, grinning.

Suddenly shy, she shrugged. "Just…this and that."

He walked across the room, slipped his arms around her waist. "Do you know how sexy this apron is?"

She chuckled. "Don't get any ideas about taking it or anything else off. The girls will be back from the honey shed any minute."

"Hadn't crossed my mind."

Laughing, she stepped from his embrace, retrieved the melted butter from the stove. "After last night?"

Skip wiggled his eyebrows. "You know me too well, bee lady."

Yesterday evening Charmaine had taken the girls to a movie while Skip and Addie spent a few hours alone. Rather than waste time driving into town, they had opted for a quiet dinner—and more—here.

Brushing a light coat of butter across the loaf tops, she said, "Did you ever think two years ago we'd be in this very spot?"

His face sobered. "You were still married then, Addie. But I never stopped wishing."

Somewhere deep inside, neither had she. Now, with their lives on the same path, she wanted more. And so did Skip. "When should we talk to the girls about renting out my house?" she asked.

Before he could respond, the front door burst open and giggles bubbled through the house. Becky and Mick had returned. Using the apron to wipe her hands, Addie headed for the foyer.

Rain dripped from the children's hair, noses and slickers. Mud coated their boots and both pairs of jeans were damp to the knees.

But, oh, those eyes! Bright with pure glee.

Fighting a grin, she took the bee-shaped honey jars from their reddened hands. "Seems you two took a few detours."

"There are millions and millions of puddles, Mom," Mick exclaimed. "It was really, really hard to walk and not step in one. Right, Bean?"

"Uh-huh. There weren't any clear spots."

"I can see that," Addie deadpanned.

Behind her, Skip laughed.

Five minutes later, dressed in dry clothes, the girls sat politely and quietly at the kitchen table, and the slices of freshly baked bread slathered in homegrown honey remained untouched on their plates.

Their glee was gone.

In its place, two somber faces cast glances at each other, then at Skip and Addie. Her stomach dipped. Had something gone amiss at the honey shed—or upstairs while they changed clothes?

"Thought you girls were hungry," Skip said, winking at Addie, trying, she knew, to ignore the sudden tension. "You're missing out." He reached for a second slice, drizzled on more honey.

Becky took Michaela's hand. "We want to ask you something."

Under the table Skip's knee nudged Addie's in support. "Shoot."

"Well," Becky began. "Me'n Mick got this idea…"

"About you, Mom." Her youngest beamed.

"And you, Dad." Again the shared glance. "You might not agree, or like it, but—" Becky hiked her chin "—*we* do."

Defiance in their eyes, they stared at Skip and Addie.

"Becky," he said, "unless you girls tell us what's on your minds, we can't make a decision."

"Okay." She inhaled hard. "We want you to marry Addie, 'cause then we can be sisters forever."

"Yeah." Michaela focused on Addie. "Sisters like you and Aunty Kat and Aunty Lee."

"Oh, girls." She felt a rush of tears. "I don't—"

"Please, Mom," Michaels blurted. "Our house is old an' ugly, an' anyways I wanna live in Becky's house so Skip can be like my dad an' you can be like Bean's mom an'—an' *everything*."

"Please, Addie." Becky's expression held a world of wishes. "I'll call you Mom if you marry Dad."

Skip shoved back his chair and went to squat between the children. "Girls, there's no requirement to call us Mom or Dad unless *you* want to. Meantime, your mom and I—" across the table his eyes captured Addie's "—would be honored to accept your request."

"You would?" Becky zeroed in on Addie.

"Oh, sweetie… Nothing would make us happier."

Cheering, the girls darted out of the chairs and around the table to hug Addie while she stared at Skip, awestruck. *Our dreams are complete,* she wanted to tell him, but the words were too thick.

His ear-to-ear grin said he understood completely.

And couldn't agree more.

Epilogue

Thanksgiving night, ten weeks later...

Addie parked herself against the counter and looked across Skip's kitchen—*their* kitchen—to where he crouched to retrieve Barbie and Ken dolls off the floor under the table. The range light's soft glow touched his dark hair with bits of gold. His pearl-gray shirt stretched across his wide shoulders and slotted tiny pleats where the cloth met his charcoal dress slacks. Loosened moments ago, his red tie hung like a pair of broad ribbons down his chest. *My husband,* she thought, wanting nothing more than to wrap her arms around him and never let go.

A few hours before, the house was full of the clamor of their families—Charmaine, Lee, Kat, Blake and Miriam Dalton—as they witnessed Addie, Skip, Michaela and Becky become their own family with the help of the local minister. To celebrate, they'd swallowed miniflutes of nonalcoholic punch, and feasted on a Thanksgiving turkey glazed in the honey from Addie's bees and cooked by Lee and Kat.

Now, with the families gone and the girls sleeping over at Kat's for the weekend, the house lay quiet with night and warmth.

Addie thought of how precious Michaela and Becky looked in their rosy-pink skirts and shoes, carrying white calla lilies to match their tops and Addie's shin-length dress. Forgoing traditional practices, their daughters had wanted to give their parents to each other. Michaela had presented Skip with Addie's ring while Becky had offered Skip's ring to Addie.

As if sensing her mood, he glanced up. "I thought," he said, voice a little raspy, "that Mick might wonder where these were when she gets home." He looked down at the dolls dressed in conventional bride and groom clothes.

Addie's heart sang. "Do you realize," she said, walking over and taking the dolls to set them on the table before casing her arms around her husband's neck, "what a wonderful father you are?"

"Well…" He tugged her against him. "I couldn't leave poor old Ken lying on the floor beside his bride. She might get the wrong impression."

Addie huffed a tiny laugh. "Not if she's thinking like this bride. Lying on the floor, lying in the grass, on the beach, in the woods, in bed…" She kissed his jaw. "Every place is perfect as long as the lying down can be with her husband."

"Every place, huh?" He took her hand, snuggled close, swayed gently to a melody only he heard. "What if all that lying down results in another little Barbie or Ken?"

"It's already happened."

He stilled. "Are you sure?" Amazement trembled in his voice.

"According to three little sticks last week and the doctor's appointment yesterday." She looked up into his dear face. "Seems we're as fertile as my queens in their hives. Do you know they can lay between fifteen hundred to three thousand eggs a day?"

"Ah, sweetheart." Laughing, Skip danced her slowly around the kitchen. "Seems you only need one around me."

She grinned. "And you're very good at doing the circle dance just like my bees. Does that mean, there's a new batch of flowers nearby?"

"Thought you'd never ask." With a kiss to her nose, he lifted her into his arms and started for the stairs to the second floor.

On the threshold of their bedroom, Skip set her down as she let out a little *oooh!* of delight.

A hundred colors exploded from two massive bouquets in crystal vases on the table in the small lounging alcove. Between the vases, champagne and two flutes chilled in a bucket of ice.

Addie's gaze moved to the big sleigh bed with its quilt of russet, gold and green. Across the pillows red, yellow and white rose petals caught the candlelight glowing from the night tables.

Skip drew her against his chest, set his chin on her hair. "One bouquet from each of the girls," he murmured, voice low and oh-so dear. "They wanted to surprise you. Lee and Kat brought the flowers upstairs, while we were getting pictures with the kids."

Her eyes stung. "Oh," she said again. "Ohhh…."

Their wedding night, adorned by the hands of her children and sisters.

Skip turned her in his arms and touched her cheek. "Addie, there will be times we don't agree. There will be times we can't agree enough. And through each and all those times I will love you." He set a hand against the flatness of her tummy. "I swear on our unborn child and the two we already have and any future children, you will be a part of me forever."

Humbled, she gazed at the freshly cut flowers spilling their scents and at the bed with its quilt of clover colors.

The room was a field of beauty and wonder and loving warmth. Joy in her heart, she took his hand and walked into the field.

* * * * *

Don't miss Lee's story,
the next chapter in Mary J. Forbes's new miniseries
HOME TO FIREWOOD ISLAND
On sale January 2009, wherever Silhouette books are sold.

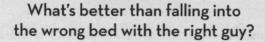

REQUEST YOUR FREE BOOKS!

2 FREE NOVELS PLUS 2 FREE GIFTS!

SPECIAL EDITION®

Life, Love and Family!

YES! Please send me 2 FREE Silhouette Speâal Edition® novels and my 2 FREE gifts (gifts are worth about $10). After receiving them, if I don't wish to receive any more books, I can return the shipping statement marked "cancel." If I don't cancel, I will receive 6 brand-new novels every month and be billed just $4.24 per book in the U.S. or $4.99 per book in Canada, plus 25¢ shipping and handling per book and applicable taxes, if any*. That's a savings of at least 15% off the cover price! I understand that accepting the 2 free books and gifts places me under no obligation to buy anything. I can always return a shipment and cancel at any time. Even if I never buy another book from Silhouette, the two free books and gifts are mine to keep forever.

235 SDN EEYU 335 SDN EEY6

Name	(PLEASE PRINT)
Address	Apt. #
City	State/Prov.	Zip/Postal Code

Signature (if under 18, a parent or guardian must sign)

Mail to the **Silhouette Reader Service**:
IN U.S.A.: P.O. Box 1867, Buffalo, NY 14240-1867
IN CANADA: P.O. Box 609, Fort Erie, Ontario L2A 5X3

Not valid to current subscribers of Silhouette Speâal Edition books.

Want to try two free books from another line?
Call 1-800-873-8635 or visit www.morefreebooks.com.

* Terms and prices subject to change without notice. N.Y. residents add applicable sales tax. Canadian residents will be charged applicable provinâal taxes and GST. This offer is limited to one order per household. All orders subject to approval. Credit or debit balances in a customer's account(s) may be offset by any other outstanding balance owed by or to the customer. Please allow 4 to 6 weeks for delivery. Offer available while quantities last.

Your Privacy: Silhouette is committed to protecting your privacy. Our Privacy Policy is available online at www.eHarlequin.com or upon request from the Reader Service. From time to time we make our lists of customers available to reputable third parties who may have a product or service of interest to you. If you would prefer we not share your name and address, please check here. ☐

SSE08

Silhouette® Desire

Cole's Red-Hot Pursuit

Cole Westmoreland is a man who gets what he wants. And he wants independent and sultry Patrina Forman! She resists him—until a Montana blizzard traps them together. For three delicious nights, Cole indulges Patrina with his brand of seduction. When the sun comes out, Cole and Patrina are left to wonder—will this be the end of the passion that storms between them?

Look for

COLE'S RED-HOT PURSUIT

by USA TODAY bestselling author

BRENDA JACKSON

Available in June 2008 wherever you buy books.

Always Powerful, Passionate and Provocative.

COMING NEXT MONTH

#1903 A MERGER...OR MARRIAGE?—RaeAnne Thayne
The Wilder Family

For Anna Wilder, it was double jeopardy—not only was she back in Walnut River to negotiate a hospital takeover her family opposed, the attorney she was up against was long-ago love interest Richard Green. Would the still-tempting single dad deem Anna a turncoat beneath contempt...or would their merger talks lead to marriage vows?

#1904 WHEN A HERO COMES ALONG—Teresa Southwick
Men of Mercy Medical

When nurse Kate Carpenter met helicopter pilot Joe Morgan in the E.R., their affair was short but very sweet...and it had consequences that lasted a lifetime. Kate had no illusions that Joe would help raise their son, especially when he hit a rough patch during an overseas deployment. Then her hero came along and surprised her.

#1905 THE MAN NEXT DOOR—Gina Wilkins

Legal assistant Dani Madison had learned her lesson about men the hard way. Or so she thought. Because her irresistible new neighbor, FBI agent Teague Carson, was about to show her that playing it safe would only take her so far....

#1906 THE SECOND-CHANCE GROOM—Crystal Green
The Suds Club

When the fire went out of his marriage, firefighter Travis Webb had to rescue the one-of-a-kind bond he had with his wife, Mei Chang Webb, and their daughter, Isobel, before it was too late. Renewing their vows in a very special ceremony seemed like a good first step in his race for a second chance.

#1907 IN LOVE WITH THE BRONC RIDER—Judy Duarte
The Texas Homecoming

Laid up after a car crash had taken all that was dear to him, rodeo cowboy Matt Clayton was understandably surly. But maid-with-a-past Tori McKenzie wasn't having it, and took every opportunity to get the bronc rider back in the saddle...and falling for Tori in a big way!

#1908 THE DADDY PLAN—Karen Rose Smith
Dads in Progress

It was a big gamble for Corrie Edwards to ask her boss, veterinarian Sam Barclay, if he'd be the sperm donor so she could have a baby. But never in her wildest dreams would she expect skeptical Sam's next move—throwing his heart in the bargain....

SSECNM0508